THE SUBMISSION FACTORY

by

BECKY BELL

I0517111

Published by **CHIMERA**
ISBN 9781780804620

Chapter One

I opened my eyes. I had been sleeping deeply and knew I had been dreaming, long convoluted dreams, but I couldn't remember a single one of them.

For a moment I thought I might still be dreaming because though I knew my eyes were open I couldn't see a thing. But when I tried to sit up and found I couldn't move I soon realised this was no dream. What felt like broad leather straps were buckled tightly around my ankles, above my knees, around my thighs and above and below my breasts, binding my arms to my sides. I couldn't even roll over because another strap around my waist was attached to either side of whatever I was lying on.

As if that wasn't disconcerting enough, I hadn't the faintest idea where I was or how I'd got there. In fact, I soon realised, the only thing I could remember was a woman, a silky-haired brunette. I had no idea who she was but I had this vivid memory of watching her slip out of a clinging red dress. Under it she had been wearing a lacy black basque and sheer black stockings, their black tops pulled taut by her suspenders, in sharp contrast to the flesh of her creamy thighs. She had slender and beautifully contoured legs and wore black high heels, and I could remember her telling me I must lie on my stomach on the floor.

That's all. Absolutely all. I searched my mind for other memories but there were none. It was as if it had been wiped clean. I could remember every detail of the brunette, the way her sleek black hair had been swept up into a chignon to reveal her elegant neck and how her big, pulpy breasts had billowed against the low cut bra of the basque. She wasn't wearing panties and her dark pubes had been trimmed neatly. The memory of her was tinged with a distinct sexual desire but, though my mind was blank, I did not find this odd because I was sure I had felt that sort of attraction for a woman before.

But who was she? More important who was I? That information was missing too.

I tried to flex my muscles against the leather straps. It was no good. The bondage was too tight. I could barely manage to rock my body from side to side. The only real movement I could accomplish was to raise and turn my head. As I experimented with this I became conscious of another sensation. I was incredibly sexually excited. Apart from the straps I was naked and my clitoris, trapped between my tightly bound thighs, was hard and throbbing. My nipples too were erect.

Considering my condition and my lack of memory I felt remarkably calm. I lay in the dark with my eyes open, and after a while detected the faintest chink of light coming from under a door. I listened for any sound but could hear nothing.

I don't know how long I lay there. It might have been an hour it might have been a minute, there was no way I could keep track of time. The image of the brunette did not fade, nor did my sexual excitement. I would have given

2

anything to be able to free my hands and touch myself. I knew it would only have taken a few brief moments with my fingers to frot my clitoris to orgasm. But I just lay thinking of the brunette's penetrating brown eyes and the way they had stared at me with an unwavering intensity.

The door opened suddenly, flooding the room with light. I screwed up my eyes but the light penetrated through my eyelids. I groaned in pain.

'She's awake.' It was a female voice.

'Good, right on schedule.' So was that.

I heard footsteps approaching the bed. I managed to open my eyes though tears still clouded my vision. For a moment I could not believe what I saw. I was lying on a narrow metal-framed bed with a thin mattress in a room with concrete walls. There was no window. Looking down at me was a slender woman dressed in a glistening black rubber catsuit. Even her head was encased in a tight rubber helmet and the only features I could see were her mouth, her big green eyes and the tiniest glimpse of her nostrils through holes in the rubber. The holes surrounding her eyes and mouth were outlined in red. The catsuit fitted her like a second skin and moulded itself to her large breasts, wasp-like waist and long legs. It had even folded into the crease of her sex.

Her fingers pulled my eyes wider open and she stared deep into them.

'She's fine. Reactions normal.'

'What's happened to me? Where am I? Who am I?' I mumbled.

'You are who we want you to be. A name will be chosen for you during the treatment. You won't be able to remember anything. That is normal. We have wiped your memory clean. From now on your life will be very different.'

I felt a weight resting next to me. Before I knew what was happening a rubber ball was forced between my lips. Straps were buckled tightly behind my head. 'No more talking now.'

I could smell a musky perfume mixed with the unmistakable aroma of rubber. The woman took my pulse.

'She's a really pretty one, isn't she?'

'Come on, we'd better do number six before we get back to her.' This was another female voice, though I couldn't see who it belonged to.

They left, closing and locking the door behind them. Once more I was plunged into darkness.

'We have wiped your memory clean.' Those words echoed in my head. Except I could still remember the brunette. I concentrated on that. I began to remember other things. I remembered being in a car. It was going very slowly in traffic. It was a big limousine and I was sitting in the back seat. I tried to remember all the details of the car. Then I realised I had been sitting next to someone, a man. I tried to see his face but it was vague and indistinct.

The car was pulling over to the side of the road. The door opened. I got out. The man got out. He led me inside a small, modern building. He was saying something but I couldn't remember what he said. It was all like a dream, fuzzy and incoherent, but slowly I began to remember more and more.

3

A door opened. It was the brunette, but this time she was fully dressed. She was smiling, kissing the man on the cheek, ushering us in. I could see her lips moving but couldn't hear what she was saying. The man was talking too. He told me to sit down.

Then I realised who he was. It was my husband. I was married. But I couldn't remember anything about the brunette. I was sure I'd never met her before. Why had my husband brought me here? Now I remember what she said. There was a sort of spinning wheel made of coloured glass and I was looking into it. I remembered more and more clearly. There was a feeling of drowsiness.

I was fighting it. She kept telling me to go to sleep. I closed my eyes and pretended I was asleep but I wasn't, not at that stage anyway. I heard the brunette tell my husband the treatment was very effective and he would see a completely different woman when it was completed. I heard him leave. After that, though I concentrated hard, I couldn't remember anything more.

I lay with my eyes open in the dark room. I searched my mind again. Why had my husband taken me to the brunette? What had she done to me?

Then it all hit me. We were supposed to be going to see a marriage counsellor. That was it. The brunette was supposed to be a marriage counsellor. I'd had an affair. I felt myself blush as I thought about it. It all came flooding back. I'd had an affair - the first time I'd ever betrayed my marriage. My husband had found out. He'd threatened to leave me. We'd had row after row until suddenly he changed his mind and said that some of what had happened was his fault, that he'd neglected me because of his obsession with work.

He wanted to try again. But even if hypnosis was part of marriage counselling I very much doubted that making me lie on the floor while the counsellor paraded in a lacy black basque was also included in the agenda. I was struggling to understand.

How I got from that room to bondage in this prison I don't know. But I knew what the woman in rubber had said was not true. If they had tried to wipe my memory of everything it had not worked. Minute by minute my memory was flooding back. I remembered all the details of my affair with Jack, the extraordinary way we met and all the things he had done to me, unconscionable things, things I had never dreamed I would like, things that made me feel deep shame and at the same time the most profound sexual pleasure.

I had to think quickly; at any moment rubber woman would return. This had to be something to do with the brunette and my husband. She'd talked about a treatment. What did that mean? The point was that if I told rubber woman she was wrong and that I had all my memories I was completely vulnerable and unable to do anything to prevent them repeating the treatment, and this time ensuring it did work. Clearly my best plan, for the moment at least, was to play along with whatever happened and look for a chance of escape.

A moment later I heard the key turn in the lock. Rubber woman returned. Again she sat on the bed beside me. My sexual excitement had not diminished.

'We are your friends,' she said. 'We are here to teach you, to help you understand.' She produced a short rubber rod about the thickness of a finger. She squeezed it between my thighs, and it began to vibrate against my clit. I did not have to fake the real pleasure I felt as the vibrations increased. The woman's other hand cupped by naked breast and squeezed it gently. Her fingers centred on my nipple and pinched. My breasts had been reddened by the constriction of the straps on either side of them and already felt incredibly sensitive, and this manipulation only increased my sexual torment.

'You see how I can make you feel?' she said.

The rubber-framed lips leant forward and while her hand continue to play with my left nipple her mouth descended to my right, sucking and nibbling.

I moaned with pleasure, wriggling against the bondage. Then quite suddenly she bit and pinched both nipples simultaneously and I felt a wave of pain. But the pain only served to intensify the pleasure emanating from my clitoris and I gasped. Rubber woman did it again, and again, and I realised I was on the brink of an orgasm. I squirmed under the effect of these excoriating sensations.

Perhaps if my memory really had been wiped this treatment would have come as a shock to me. But it hadn't. In fact I remembered perfectly well that this was not the first time I'd experienced this unique blend of pleasure and pain. It's what Jack, my lover, had done to me; taught me what I loved, needed, craved. This is what had transformed my sex life from a repetitive chore to a mind-blowing and profound need.

I arched my body against the leather straps and knew the feeling of being in bondage, of being completely powerless to stop the woman doing whatever she wanted to do to me, was only increasing my excitement. As she bit and pinched my nipples again and the vibrations from the rod seemed to increase, I shuddered to an astonishing climax.

'You see what I can do for you?' she said.

She knelt on the bed and straddled my shoulders. I found myself staring up into her crotch. The shiny black rubber parted to reveal a slit from the top of her mons right around to her anus. The area had been assiduously depilated and I could see the crinkled flesh of her labia. The mouth of her vagina parted and I saw the scarlet wet flesh inside.

There was little doubt what she was going to do. I knew it wouldn't be my first taste of a woman, and Jack was responsible for introducing me to my own bisexuality. I'd had no idea I could get sexual pleasure from another woman until he insisted I had sex with one while he watched.

She lowered herself onto my mouth, then wriggled her hips so her sex was smeared across my face. I could do nothing but inhale the intoxicating scent. As much as I would have liked to kiss and lick her the gag prevented me. I felt my clitoris throb. Jack had awoken my submissive fantasies, feelings that, before we'd met, I didn't even want to admit to myself that I had. My bondage now was more extreme than anything he'd applied, but that only made it more exciting.

She pulled back slightly and a finger slipped between her labia. Sweat was running off my forehead and my heart was pounding, but I could not take my eyes off her finger as it nudged her clitoris from side to side. In moments she was gasping with pleasure as she came.

She moved forward again until her wet sex was pressed against the gag, then laughed and got to her feet. Without another word she turned and left the room. The door closed.

I realised my whole body was bathed in sweat. I lay alone again inhaling the strong odours of her sex, and my own, mixed inextricably together. My heartbeat slowed. My nipples ached from the pinching they had taken, but nothing diminished my sexual excitement and I could feel my thighs slick with my juices.

I looked around the room. The only light was from a naked bulb hanging from the ceiling. I expected it to be turned off at any moment. The walls were painted grey and the floor was linoleum. The only furniture was the single bed, a wooden chair and a glass-fronted cabinet. One wall had two sturdy metal rings bolted into it above head height, and there were two more at floor level. There were also ominous-looking chains hanging from the ceiling.

It was not easy to keep track of time and I don't know how long I was left like this. My thoughts turned to Jack, to what he had done to me, and what he had made me feel and the ultimate humiliation when my husband found us together. The trouble was I couldn't regret what I had done with him. I had never experienced such heights of passion. I remembered the beautiful brunette too. I remembered her walking towards me, her nylons rasping. I was looking straight into her eyes. The only gap in my memory was what she had done to me, and how I ended up here. Whatever it was I knew my husband had been behind it. I discovered I could just manage to rub my thighs together, which produced a wave of sexual feelings. I could easily bring myself off again, but I refrained. I had the feeling I was being watched and didn't want anyone to know just how turned on I was.

The door opened again. Two women entered; the original figure and another in an identical outfit, though she was shorter and had smaller breasts. I could see there was a slit in the rubber between her legs too, and I could glimpse her sex lips. Unlike her companion she was not shaved, and had black pubes.

She unbuckled the belts at my ankles, knees and thighs, leaving my arms bound while her companion undid the strap that held me to the bed. The gag was eased out, then without a word they strode back to the door and left again. The shorter one came back a moment later with two metal bowls. She placed them on the floor by the door, then shut and locked it again.

I struggled to sit up. Oddly, despite being bound so tightly for I don't know how long, I felt no real pain. There was a dull ache in my muscles but it wasn't at all unpleasant.

I realised I was starving hungry and the bowls must contain food. I managed to get to my feet but nearly fell over I was so shaky on my legs. Rather than risking toppling over without the use of my hands to break my fall, I got to my knees and crawled over to the bowls. There was water in one and a sort of stew in the other. I ate with difficulty, almost overbalancing as I snuffled in the bowl trying to catch the meat between my lips. Drinking was even more difficult.

The extraordinary thing was that even this humiliation did not diminish my profound excitement, my juices seeping down between my thighs.

The large swimming pool glistened in the night like a huge diamond, its blue mosaic tiles lit by underwater lights. A five-piece band played on the vast terrace where every shrub and tree had been draped with tiny white lights. The guests, men in evening dress, women in fabulous creations of silk, satin and lace, talked or danced or helped themselves to food from three tables groaning with delicacies. On one there were plates of oysters, pates, cold lobster, smoked salmon, salads and caviar in silver bowls surrounded by crushed ice. On another were hot dishes. The third, surmounted by an ice sculpture of a dolphin, held magnificent displays of the art of patisserie, tarts in every colour and flavour, chocolate roulades and crystal bowls of crème Chantilly and crème anglais and, at the very end a collection of French cheeses under a vast thermostatic cloche.

Barbara Harrison surveyed the scene with dismay. She hated parties. But her husband had just signed a contract worth over a hundred million euros to supply the Federation de France Nord and she could not get out of attending the celebrations. She watched her husband, Anthony, talking animatedly to Jeanne Christophe Brichot, the Managing Director of FFN. A rousse he had called her when Barbara had introduced them, the French expression, apparently, for a redhead, and Barbara was definitely that, her hair the colour of beech trees in autumn.

'Hi!'

She looked around. A man had appeared at her side. He was tall with a broad chest, a chiselled chin, black curly hair and piercing brown, almost black eyes. He exuded calm confidence and superiority.

'Hello,' she said.

'You're Barbara Harrison. I've been watching you.'

'Have you? Why's that?'

'I've seen your pictures in the papers,' he said.

'Since my picture is only ever in the financial press standing beside my husband you must be some sort of investment consultant.'

'No. But I like to know what's going on. My name's Jack, by the way. Jack Harkness.'

'Pleased to meet you Jack.'

A waiter passed with a tray of champagne and Jack stopped him.

'Your glass is empty. And don't say you're driving. You've got a chauffeur-driven Rolls outside.' He took two of the tall flutes, handing her one. 'Do you fancy going for a little walk? It's a lovely evening isn't it?'

'All right.'

She wasn't at all sure why - perhaps it was the feeling that her husband was neglecting her - but she let him take her arm and led her to a path through a long avenue of shrubs. The noise of the music gradually receded.

'I love that dress.'

Barbara was wearing a startling black sleeveless gown with a high neckline. But the front of the dress was slashed from neck to waist, the opening highlighted with silver thread, and revealed a great deal of her pliant and unencumbered breasts. She had always been proud of her breasts. They were full and firm and did not need the help of a bra. The man's eyes were examining every available inch of them.

'You seem to know a lot about me.'

'I know you are the most attractive woman at this party. Oh yes, you asked me why I've been watching you. Well that's the reason.'

'I'm married.'

'Does that mean you are not interested in a little adventure?'

'Are you trying to seduce me?'

'I'm trying to tell you that I know what you need.'

'Listen, I'm flattered but I've never cheated on my husband.'

The path led away from the house down to a block of garages and workshops. A little further on was a stable and a stable yard lit by tall wrought-iron lamps. He stopped by a slender tree. One of the shafts of light fell across his face and Barbara could not help thinking there was a sort of raw power about the man which she found terribly attractive.

'You've never had really mind-blowing sex with him either, have you?'

'That's none of your business,' she said. She had meant it to come out angrily but it didn't. The truth was what he said had touched a nerve. Sex had always been a problem in her marriage. Her husband preferred business adventures to sexual ones. She faked orgasms when he made love to her but her only real sexual pleasure came from a realistically moulded vibrator on full power, when she was alone.

'But I know why.'

'Why?' she asked.

'Because he doesn't give you want you need. And I can.'

'Oh, can you?' That didn't come out right either. She intended it to sound sceptical and mocking. But it came out as more of a question.

'Believe me. I have a special talent. I know exactly what a woman needs even when sometimes she doesn't know it herself.'

He had won the first round. She was intrigued. 'And what do I need?'

'Give me your hands.' He said it in quite a different tone of voice, sharp and so dominant it took her by surprise and she meekly held out her hands. He pulled them up over her head and towards a branch of the tree. She heard something click and felt a cold loop around her wrists, and when he let go she found her arms were stretched above her and she had to stand on tiptoe. To her amazement the position gave her a surge of sexual excitement quite unlike

8

anything she had felt before.

'Got you,' he said.

'What the hell do you think you're doing?' Looking up she caught the glint of light on the handcuffs around her wrists.

He wrapped his arms around her, her breasts pressing against his chest. She could smell his musky aftershave.

'Tell me you want to be free and I'll let you go,' he whispered in her ear, making her shiver.

'I...' Barbara was just about to tell him to do just that when she hesitated. The sexual excitement took her breath away.

Jack smiled. 'You see.'

He kissed her neck and her ear with delicate pecks and squirmed his belly against hers. She felt his erection beginning to grow. His hands were inching up the tight skirt of her dress until it was gathered around her waist.

'Let me go,' she said, but with no conviction.

'This is what you want, Barbara. I told you I have a talent for knowing.'

A hand was cupping her firm buttocks. She felt him grasp the silk of her panties and begin to pull them down over the tops of her sheer hold-up stockings.

'No,' she said.

'Tell me you mean that and I'll cut you loose,' he whispered. 'Come on, all you have to do is say it.'

She opened her mouth, but once again no words came out. The truth was her excitement was only increasing. She could feel her clitoris convulsing and her juices seeping. Almost without thinking she strained against the handcuffs, not because she wanted to escape but because the feeling of being tied and helpless excited her so much. Jack had discovered her innermost secret; the sexual river that had always run deep in her psyche. She had always fantasised about being submissive. It was not a rape fantasy but something else, something quite different. What she wanted was to be a slave, totally and absolutely committed to obey. It was a fantasy she'd often used on lonely nights when her husband worked late and she used her vibrator and a bottle of massage oil for sexual fulfilment, the word 'master' on her lips as she trembled to a climax.

'This is what you want,' Jack whispered.

He had pulled her panties from around her ankles and bunched them into a ball. He stuffed them into her mouth.

'Don't want the whole party to hear,' he said.

He grabbed her by the waist with one arm and smacked her left buttock. Before she could even register the pain in one cheek he began on the other, spanking her fast but hard, alternating from one buttock to the other so the whole of her backside burned. She squealed, but only a muffled moan escaped the gag.

She soon realised what she was feeling in her buttocks was not only pain. The most extraordinary thing was happening to her. The spanking generated heat and the heat turned inward, travelling directly to her sex and creating sensations she had never felt before. As each new stroke landed that feeling became more intense and more recognisably sexual. She had stopped squealing and was now moaning in undisguised delight. She was so turned on she thought she might come.

The spanking stopped. Jack knelt in front of her. He parted her thighs and draped them over his shoulders. She felt his tongue slide into her sex. Her pubic hair was already wet. With unerring accuracy he found her clit and wriggled his tongue against it. At the same time his hand moved down over her heated buttocks, deliberately caressing them to produce new shards of that delicious melange of pain and pleasure. She gasped again, unable to stop trembling.

His hand slipped between her legs and she felt his fingers at the mouth of her vagina. However much she would like to pretend to him that she was not enjoying the experience her body betrayed her. As his tongue continued to play at her clit he slid two then three fingers into her vagina. It was enough. She went rigid. Her clitoris spasmed against his mouth and she came, only just managing not to scream. She could never remember coming so intensely.

But he was not finished with her. Standing up he pulled his trousers and pants to his knees revealing a hard, handsome cock.

He pulled the panties out of her mouth then kissed her, his tongue plunging between her lips just as forcefully as his fingers had done in her sex. Barbara melted as his erection butted against her stomach. Despite the fact she had just had an orgasm she didn't think she had ever wanted a man more.

'Say it,' he said.

'Say what?'

'Tell me what you want.'

'You know.'

'Tell me,' he insisted.

'Fuck me,' she moaned against his lips.

'Again.'

'Fuck me, you evil bastard.'

He pulled away. For a moment she saw a fleeting smile on his lips; a smug, victorious smile. Then he slid his hands under her thighs and lifted her bodily, pulling her legs around his waist. Her weight was supported on the cuffs, the metal biting into her flesh, but she felt nothing but excitement as his cock nudged between her thighs.

'Perhaps I should get back to the party,' he said teasingly, holding his cock at the entrance to her vagina.

'No, no,' she cried in alarm.

'If you want it you're going to have to beg for it,' he said.

'Please, please, fuck me.'

For a moment he did nothing. The heat from his cock spread upward into her sex. Her clitoris seemed to be on fire. She tried to move down to trap his cock but the position, hanging from the branch of the tree, made it impossible for her

10

to do anything but hope the obvious heat and wetness of her sex would draw him in. She knew he was showing her that she was completely in his power, and that excited her too.

'This is what you want, isn't it?'

At that moment he thrust up into her, his cock lunging all the way up until his glans was lodged at the neck of her womb. In reaction her sex contracted around him as tightly as a fist. She seemed to be able to feel every throbbing vein of his cock, every inch of it. It filled her completely. Her sex relaxed momentarily then contracted again and her clitoris seemed to explode, throwing her into an orgasm as deep and intense as the one before. She had never come so quickly in her life.

He hadn't finished with her. Not giving her any chance to come down from the highs he began to thrust into her, strong thrusts as his hands grasped her thighs. Just as she felt herself coming down from one orgasm this produced another. She moaned and came again, each thrust taking her to new heights.

Eventually he stopped. She felt him leaving her body and saw his erection glistening with her juices in the light from the stables.

'What do you want?' she managed to pant.

As if to answer he reached up and freed her hands from the handcuffs then pressed on her shoulders, wanting her to kneel. As she sunk to her knees his cock was inches from her mouth.

'Suck it,' he ordered. She obeyed at once, gripping his shaft in one hand and sucking as hard as she could. She tasted her own juices. She wanted desperately to feel it pushing into her throat but that was not what he had in mind. She felt his glans throb and knew he was going to come. She wanted his spunk in her mouth, but instead, as his cock jerked wildly he pulled out and ejaculated over her lips and face and into her dishevelled hair.

As the viscous liquid slid over her face she used her tongue to gather up what she could, licking and swallowing as if it were some special nectar.

'I told you I had a special talent,' he said, his lips parting in a smile.

Chapter Two

The most annoying thing was not being able to wipe my mouth after I had eaten. I didn't want to foul the water by using it to wash in because I might want to drink it later, so I crawled back to the bed and managed to wipe my lips on the mattress. After my experiences with Jack I knew why being bound so tightly in this anonymous room and being humiliated by being fed like a dog turned me on so much.

The door opened again. The two rubber-clad women strode into the room.

'On the floor,' the taller of the two said.

I did not understand. I was already on my knees.

'When a mistress enters the room it is necessary that you prostrate yourself on the floor on your belly,' she said in a tone that suggested she was speaking to a wayward child.

Those words opened another door in my memory. The brunette had said that to me. I could see her beautiful lips moving as she'd pronounced the words. I looked down at the leather straps sealing my arms to my sides and tried to work out how I could manage to lower myself to the floor without doing myself an injury.

The taller of the two strode over to me. She had a strip of leather in her hand. Its end was split into three tails. She raised her arm and I watched helplessly as the strap sliced across my breasts. They exploded with pain and I yelped.

'You will always do as you're told immediately,' she said. Her attitude was stern and severe, completely different from the last time she had come into the room.

There was only one way to accomplish what she wanted, so I braced myself and toppled sideways, then rolled onto my stomach.

'This is called position number one. You are required to remember that,' the shorter woman said.

The taller one stood in front of my face. 'Lick my shoes, both of them.'

I raised my head and licked. It was odd that despite everything I had a strong desire to obey whatever I was told to do. What was even stranger was that humiliating myself in this way gave me a distinct jolt of excitement. As I licked I felt the buckles on the leather straps around my body being freed.

'Stand up.'

After having been trapped for so long my arms felt as if they were made from rubber, but I managed to struggle to my feet. Even if I had wanted to try and escape my muscles were so atrophied they would have no trouble in overpowering me.

'You will address me as Madam Celine.' The taller one said. 'This is Madam Angel.'

'Who am I?' I thought I should at least try to maintain the illusion that I knew nothing.

'No questions.' The leather tawse snaked out and caught my breast again. There was the same stinging pain followed by a pulse of hot pleasure. I couldn't work out whether the pain was worth the pleasure that followed.

Angel had gone back out. She returned with an armful of chains and leather straps. She dropped them on the bed. Both picked up a leather cuff which they buckled around my wrists. The cuffs had a steel D-ring set into them. They applied two more sets to my arms just above my elbow, and to my ankles.

I wanted to ask what they were going to do with me, but I did not want another taste of the tawse. They stood on the chair to attach chains to hooks set in the ceiling, then used spring-loaded clips to attach the D-rings on the wrist cuffs to them so I was standing in the middle of the room with both arms up and out above my head. They pulled my legs apart and attached the ankle cuffs to either end of a metal bar, forcing my legs apart so I was spread-eagled.

12

I was deeply excited by this bondage. I was unable to do anything to stop whatever they wanted to do to me, to the most intimate parts of me, but that only made my pulse race. Since I'd met Jack it always had.

Celine stood in front of me, her face inches from mine. Her eyes were hard and cruel. She cupped my left breast, caressing it gently, then let her hand slide down to my tummy. I was deeply ashamed that she would find clear evidence of my excitement, but there was nothing I could do to stop her. Slowly her fingers worked their way into my sex.

'She's soaking wet,' she reported to her colleague.

'They always are,' Angel said. She came over and I saw an aerosol can in her hand. She knelt down beside me and began spraying between my legs. I looked down and was able to see a thick white mousse, rather like whipped cream, covering my pubic hair. Though it was cold it was not an unpleasant sensation. Not immediately at least. After two or three minutes I felt an itching that was soon replaced by a feeling of being burnt. I struggled against my bondage, trying to free my hands so I could wipe it away. The heat increased. The tender flesh of my labia was on fire.

I saw the women smiling at my discomfort.

'Please...' I begged, tearing my limbs against the cuffs.

'Five minutes and we wipe it away,' Madam Celine said. 'Have to do a proper job.'

The heat seemed to be spreading, not out across my thighs but inward as if the mousse had invaded my vagina. It was changing too, into a different type of heat; sexual heat. My clitoris began to throb and I felt my juices run. Instead of pulling against my bondage I began squirming in it, trying to bring my thighs together to put pressure on my clit. It was useless. My legs were bound too far apart.

'It always has that effect,' Madam Angel said. I saw her take a towel and she began to wipe the mousse away. When she rubbed it against my clit I thought I was going to come. The mousse had removed my hair.

Madam Celine examined my labia closely. 'No, she doesn't need another go. There wasn't much more than bum-fluff there anyway. Why don't we give her a little treat?'

Angel smiled. She knelt on the floor then pushed her mouth against my sex. Her tongue parted my labia, searching for my clit. I moaned as the tip touched the little button of nerves. The heat of the depilation cream had left me hungry for sex.

But exactly as before the rush of pleasure was followed by an equal and equivalent wave of pain. A thin line of heat burned across my buttocks and I yelped. I squirmed my head around to see Madam Celine standing behind me with a thin cane in her hand.

Madam Angel's tongue prodded at my clit. The heat from my buttocks felt like a thousand needles had been pressed into my flesh and I tried to ease the pain by wriggling my hips from side to side. This also had the effect of smearing my clitoris against Madam Angel's tongue, producing a delicious sensation. The pain in my buttocks turned inwards, the heated blood coursing into my sex.

'That feels so good, doesn't it?' Celine said.

'No, no, not again.' I begged even though I was deliberately pushing my sex against Madam Angel's tongue. I felt a wave of wet pleasure engulf me as my clit reacted to the provocation.

'Pleasure and pain,' Celine said. She raised her arm and whipped the cane down onto my buttocks. Again I felt the burning line explode across my arse, pain that made me scream. She stroked it down three times in quick succession until my bum felt as if it were on fire and I was pulling desperately against my bondage to find some way to escape. This again had the effect of wriggling my sex against Madam Angel's mouth my labia pressed against her lips. As the pain receded I felt her slide the tip of her tongue against my clit again, but this time her fingers probed then thrust up into my sex.

The pain in my buttocks again seemed to be turning into another different sensation. There was no doubt in my mind that it was intensifying the pleasure. I was totally confused, not because my body responded to this sort of treatment but that, once again, I found it hard to understand why I was prone to a masochism so deeply embedded that it could bring me with such rapidity, as if had with Jack, to the point of orgasm. Desperately I squirmed against Angel's mouth and tried to press myself down on her fingers.

But it was another sensation that took me over the top and plunging down into an abyss of bliss. As I felt Angel's tongue worming on my clit and her fingers fucking my sex Madam Celine's cool hand cupped by buttocks, caressing the weals the cane had left there. I couldn't separate the pain from the pleasure, they were simply one rush of sensation. I found myself quivering from head to toe as my orgasm shook through my body. Even in the midst of these shuddering sensations I realised that being bound and spread so helplessly, not even able to touch my own sex, had added another level to my orgasm. It was a good job I was held so firmly in bondage because I don't know how I would have managed to stay on my feet after such a sensory assault.

As I recovered my senses, hanging limply from the leather cuffs, a new need asserted itself. Even after such a wild climax I found my sex aching for the feeling of a cock thrusting into me. I was turned on by sex with a woman, but I still wanted a man. The thought of it made my sex spasm and I couldn't suppress a moan.

'Come here,' Celine said to Angel. 'You know how doing this turns me on.'

I watched as Celine sat on the bed and opened her legs, the rubber parting to reveal her shaved sex. I could see she was glistening with her juices. Angel knew what was required of her. She knelt on the floor in front of Celine, who raised her legs and draped them over Angel's shoulders. As Celine's high heels dug into her back Angel pressed her mouth to the woman's sex, just as she had to mine moments before.

Celine gasped. Angel moved her head from side to side and I could hear sucking noises. Celine fell back across the bed, her head lolling over the other side as she started making little squeals of pleasure. The squeals turned to the sort of cries I heard as she'd sat on my face. I saw her rubber-covered limbs stretched taut. My clit throbbed as I watched the two women together.

Angel stopped, but did not pull away until Celine had recovered and sat up. Then both women got to their feet.

They unclipped my wrists from the chains and my ankles were freed from the metal bar. They forced my arms behind my back. Both the wrists and the elbow cuffs were then clipped together, straining my shoulders back and my breasts forward. A leather collar was buckled around my neck and a chain fitted to it, like a dog leash. I had been made to eat like a dog now, apparently, I was to be led around like one.

I was made to sit on the bed and Madam Celine drew the sheerest black stockings over my legs, stretching them until every wrinkle had been removed. Then they pulled me up and eased my feet into black high heels; the heels so high my feet were almost vertical and I found myself tottering, unable to use my arms for balance. Madam Angel gripped my shoulders to steady me.

Angel picked up a leather blindfold. She fitted it over my eyes and strapped it tightly at the back of my head. There was thick padding on the inside which made it impossible for me to see anything. I was plunged back into a world of darkness.

'Open your mouth,' Celine said.

I felt a ball being forced inside, pushing my tongue down and making it impossible for me to close my lips. It was strapped in place, two going around my head and one going vertically up over the centre of my head to meet the other straps at the back. It had apparently had been designed to accommodate my nose.

I felt a pull from the leash. I walked forward tentatively, finding it hard to balance on the shoes. After a few steps I felt the texture of the floor change. It felt like stone or tile. It is a very unpleasant sensation to be pulled along in complete darkness with your arms tied behind your back and no idea where you are and what you might bump into. I mistook my step several times and received a sharp slap of what I was sure was the tawse across my buttocks. I had to trust the women to warn me of any obstacle.

We walked for some minutes, turning left and right. The texture of the floor changed again. From the clack of the high heels on it this was definitely wood.

'Stop.'

I felt someone pull my wrists up, forcing me to bend forward. I was pushed backward and felt my arms being pulled over some sort of support which rested under my shoulders. As my wrist cuffs were tugged downward and I straightened up again I heard a clink of metal as they were secured to what felt like a post running the whole way down my back. My legs were forced apart and something was attached to the ankle cuffs so I could not close them and my sex was exposed. In this position I was arched up and my breasts forced out, the strain on the muscles of my arms and back creating an acute pain. Whatever was under my arms was solid and supported my weight.

I became aware of a musky perfume. I started as a hand ran over my left breast. It circled both of them then caressed my shamefully hard nipples so tenderly I could not help but moan.

'She's very sensitive.' A man's voice, the first I had heard since I'd woken up. Disorientated by being bound, gagged and blindfolded, let alone by my shattering orgasms at the hands of two women, I did not recognise it immediately. But when I did I was glad I had been gagged and blindfolded otherwise I'm sure I would not have been able to stop myself from giving the game away. The voice belonged to my husband, Tony.

Whether it was the same hand that then pinched by nipples one by one, twisting them, I did not know. I felt fingers caressing my thighs above the stockings. I realised there was nothing I could do to prevent the hand penetrating me or doing anything else it wanted to pleasure or torture me. I was powerless.

'Let's get on with it,' Tony said. I could hear excitement in his voice.

I listened intently. I had the impression there were other people in the room too, though no one said anything. I wondered if one of them was the brunette. I don't know why but I couldn't get rid of the idea that I was the centre of attention and that they had come to see whatever was going to happen to me.

I felt a hand slide down between my open legs. It was coating my labia with something slippery and warm. It cupped by sex then worked from my anus to my clit. It was the most delicious sensation. Even after my orgasm I felt myself preparing for another.

I should have learnt my lesson. Pleasure and pain, isn't that what they said? I felt a sharp pain burn through my left nipple. I knew immediately what they'd done. I'd felt the same pain before when I'd had my ears pierced. They'd pierced my nipple. Something cold was being passed through it. The shock of it almost took my breath away.

The hand had not stopped moving up and down my sex on the lubricant it had applied. I tried to brace myself for the pain that would inevitably occur again, but the hand was too persuasive. I felt my clit swelling and my orgasm blossoming once more.

I gasped into the gag as the same intense pain speared through my right nipple. At the same moment my orgasm exploded from my clit. What I had experienced with Jack had been the beginning of a voyage of discovery I had taken in my own psyche, and my response to what I was experiencing now showed how far I had come on that journey. There was no doubt in my mind that the extreme bondage and whatever they had used on my nipples had provoked an orgasm off the scale of anything I'd felt before.

The hand moved away. I felt juices leaking from my open sex and I was unable to control my body from trembling like a leaf. Both my nipples were on fire. I ached to touch them and soothe them and tried to move my hands though I knew I could not. As if reading my mind something cold and slightly astringent was wiped over both nipples, making me gasp, the sharp pain suddenly renewed as well as the pleasure that went with it.

I had no idea what the purpose of all this was or where it would end, but whatever it was if it involved such sexual satisfaction I didn't care. This was what I had always wanted. This was who I was and who I am.

'The pain becomes quickly associated with pleasure,' a woman said. It was not the voice of Angel or Celine but I'd heard it before. It was the brunette. 'Surprisingly quickly. And that is absolutely necessary to the process.'

'Why is that?' Tony asked.

'Because slaves have to be punished frequently. They must suffer real pain. But they must also want that pain and it must excite them sexually so that they are in the right frame of mind to be useful to their masters and their masters' guests.'

'Oh course, how clever. But can you do that with anyone?'

'No, definitely not. There has to be a natural inclination to submission.'

'And we know she has that in spades,' Tony said, naturally enough, considering the way he had found me with Jack. And of course that was why my nipples had been pierced. He had remembered what I'd said that terrible night he'd found us together. And here I was again, bound, gagged and blindfolded, the truth of what he had just said perfectly obvious by the state I was in. More than ever I knew I'd made the right decision to play along and see exactly what would transpire.

'Perhaps we should have put one through her nose too,' he mused.

'That can be arranged.'

There was laughter.

'I like her shaved like that,' he said.

'That's what you asked for,' the woman replied. 'From now on you make all the decisions of how she looks and behaves. Some of the masters even go so far as to shave their heads.'

Again I was glad I was gagged. That remark would have certainly made me exclaim with horror. It was becoming increasingly obvious that the 'treatment' I'd heard them talking about was intended to reduce me to a role of an unquestioning slave.

I heard several pairs of high heels leaving the room. I felt the blindfold being unstrapped. When I opened my eyes the room was deserted apart from Madam Angel. It was a large square room with a polished wooden floor that looked a little like a small gymnasium. My arms were pulled over the top of a T-shaped frame and my ankles were clipped to metal rings set in the floor. Extending from my breasts and up to a ring in the ceiling were two thin wires. I looked down, and saw they were tied to two gold rings that pierced my nipples and pulled my breasts upward!

'Don't you look pretty,' Madam Angel purred.

Chapter Three

'Why didn't you answer any of my calls?' she said angrily.

'Because I didn't feel like it.'

'I thought you wanted me.'

'Perhaps I changed my mind.'

He had tucked a little white card with gold lettering into the waistband of her panties as he pulled them up around her hips on the night of the party. She had been trying his number for days and always got the answerphone. She'd left dozens of messages.

After the FFN party Barbara had tried to pretend to herself that she didn't want to see Jack Harkness again. But she couldn't stop thinking about him and what he had done to her. Her sex life prior to the party had become a diminuendo of inactivity. Her husband seemed very little inclined to make love to her and when he did it was a matter of routine, the same position, the same brief foreplay and the same even briefer penetration culminating in his orgasm and very, very rarely in hers. She would masturbate lazily once every five or six days with a vibrator, but hadn't really felt any urgency or inclination to do more.

But now all that had changed. Since the party she had become acutely aware of sex. She had been unable to prevent herself from feeding her biggest dildo deep into her vagina and making herself come, sometimes as often as three times a day. Each time it was the vivid, almost photographic memory of what Jack had said and done to her that was running through her mind as her orgasm exploded. Each time her orgasm was of the same intensity, even when it was the second or third of the day. What happened at the party was the most erotic experience she'd ever had, and in the end she decided there was no point in denying that.

Today she'd already called him three times and was almost surprised when finally, at six o'clock, he answered the phone. His rich voice made her shiver.

'Can I come and see you?' she asked. She tried to make her tone more conciliatory, afraid that her anger would backfire and he'd put the phone down.

'What for?'

'Jack, please...'

'I'll expect you in an hour, and don't be late,' he said in an irritable tone. Leaving no room for discussion he hung up.

Barbara was supposed to be going to a dinner of the Society of Metal Manufacturers at the guildhall with her husband. She would be missed but there was no doubt in her mind that if she had a chance to see Jack again she was going to grasp it with both hands. The chauffeur was waiting downstairs to take her to the office where she was supposed to meet Tony, so she phoned and told him she wasn't going to the dinner and he should go and pick up her husband at the office. Then she phoned Tony. Fortunately she had an excuse; her friend

Mary was ill and she told him she felt she had to go and help her get her supper. He sounded cross but that was nothing new.

She quickly ran upstairs and rifled through her lingerie draw looking for something provocative to put on. She wanted Jack to see her looking like a whore. She selected a red satin basque and black stockings with a red seam, which she'd bought when first married. In those days she'd always worn something seductive for her husband, frequently greeting him at the front door in it, when he got back from work. It usually had the desired effect, often getting him so excited they'd never even made it to the bedroom. Those days were long gone. She fastened the basque, smoothed on the silky stockings then pulled on a simple black dress and her highest black heels. She didn't bother with panties. They were, she hoped, surplus to requirements.

Half an hour later she got a cab and had it drop her off at the corner of Kensington High Street and Melbury Road. According to the address on her card Jack lived in a mansion block. She found it easily and rang the highly polished button on the panel of buttons on the entry-phone. The lock on the front door buzzed and she pushed her way inside.

The building had a peculiar smell of wax polish mixed with an underlying hint of damp. She travelled up in the lift to the sixth floor. She tried to calm herself but her heart was pumping in her chest and her hands were sweating. She found his flat and rang the doorbell. Almost before she'd lowered her hand the door burst open.

'You're late,' he said angrily.

He stood in the doorway wearing a red silk robe tied at the waist. His legs and feet were bare.

'You'd better come in. I haven't got time for this.'

'I'm sorry I just...' She couldn't think of what to say.

'I was just getting dressed.'

He closed the door and strode off down the long corridor, his naked feet slapping on the wooden parquet floor. She wasn't sure whether she should follow him or not.

'Come on,' he said irritably.

She hurried after him. He had turned into a room at the end. She followed him and found herself in a large bedroom. There was a bank of wardrobes down one side and a large double bed covered with a cream counterpane.

'So what do you want exactly, Barbara?' he said. He took off his robe. He was naked underneath. His body, which she realised she had never seen before, was coated with fine black hairs, his stomach flat and, like the rest of his body, muscular. His pubes were dense and his cock circumcised. He went to the wardrobe and began taking out some clothes.

'I thought we needed to talk.'

'About what?'

'About what happened between us?'

'You told me you didn't have affairs.'

19

'I don't. You were... just... you were so...' She couldn't think of the right thing to say.

'Spit it out.'

She looked at his naked body and felt a surge of desire. What she actually wanted to say to him was that the sexual experience at the party haunted her, that she had been unable to think about anything else, that she still shuddered every time she thought about it and that for the last two days her sex had seemed to be on fire with need.

'Go back to your husband, perhaps he'll give you what you want, if you ask him nicely.'

'I want you.'

He turned to face her, throwing the trousers he was holding on a chair.

'No, you want what I can give you,' he said.

He strode over to the chest of drawers at his bedside, opened the top drawer and took out a pair of metal handcuffs. They jangled as he held them up.

'This is what you want, this is what you're panting for. Well isn't it?'

'No... I mean...' The words would just not come out right, but she knew what he said was true. She didn't want to admit to herself that the sight of the handcuffs dangling from his hand made her sex pulse.

'Turn around.'

'No,' she said. Her heart began to pound again. Roughly he grabbed her hands, pulled them behind her back and clipped the handcuffs around her wrists.

'There, that's much better.'

She didn't understand. She could have resisted him but she didn't. Her clit was throbbing and she could hardly breathe she was so excited.

In seconds he had reduced her to a quivering mass of expectation. No man had ever made her feel like this.

Jack stood in front of her. His cock had hardened and was now pointing at the ceiling. She couldn't take her eyes off it.

'What are you looking at?' he said.

'You're very attractive.'

'What I need from you Barbara is action, not words. Kneel.'

Barbara felt another sharp pulse deep in her sex. That word and the way he said it excited her. She dropped to her knees in front of him.

'That's better.'

'Now how many do you think you deserve?'

'I don't know what you're talking about,' she said meekly.

'You know what you want, Barbara, don't pretend to me. The party was just the beginning for you, just a taste. I know why you've come here. Didn't I tell you that I have this special talent for knowing? I know everything about you. We're going to start with six. If you are not perfectly obedient I will double it.'

She shook her head as if to try and clear her thoughts. She had no idea what he was talking about. 'Please, I don't...'

'Be quiet,' he snapped. 'Pull your dress up to your waist. Can you at least do that much? Then I want your forehead pressed down on the carpet. Do I make myself clear?'

She didn't understand at all, but struggled to obey. It was terribly difficult to grip her dress with her hands locked behind her but after several attempts she managed to get it up around her waist. Then she rocked forward until her forehead was touching the carpet and her buttocks were raised.

He walked around her examining her bottom, the basque and stockings.

'Do you usually go around in such fancy lingerie?'

'No.'

'So you wore it for me, did you?'

She didn't reply. She realised this was what she wanted. She was wanton now. She knew in this position he would be able to see her sex and was glad she had decided not to wear panties. She hoped he would grab her by the hips and take her just as he had done at the party, and angled herself up towards him to show how willing she was. She even eased her knees apart so he would have a better view, her sex lips already glistening with the juices she could feel seeping from her vagina.

But he had something else in mind. From her upside down prospective she saw him walking across the room. He took something from a cupboard but she could not tell what it was. He walked back to her.

'Are you ready?'

'I don't understand...' The sentence was cut short by a whistle of air and a thwack as the riding crop landed across her buttocks. She screamed. She felt a line of pain explode across her rear; stinging pain that brought tears to her eyes. But the sensation was not just pain; deep inside her sex it provoked an entirely new reaction, a sexual sensation she had only felt once before.

Thwack. Thwack. Thwack. The blows came quickly, the combination of pain and sexual arousal so strong her whole body was trembling. He had said six. There were two more strokes to go. She dreaded them, but at the same time she wanted them.

'Shall I go on?'

He was teasing her, making her wait.

'Yes,' she muttered.

'Beg me?'

'Please, please...'

Thwack. Thwack. The last blow fell exactly on the line of scarlet red that the first had created. She cried out and rolled onto her side. She knew she was coming and knew there was no way of hiding it from him. As she lay on the floor of his bedroom, her body rolled into a ball, she moaned as the most extraordinary orgasm flowed over her.

'Now let's see if you can improve on that pathetic performance you gave at the party. Get over here.' His voice was cold and unsympathetic.

He sat on the bed and spread his legs apart. She was glad to see his cock had grown fully erect and had a tear of fluid at its tip. She was glad because she desperately wanted to excite him as much as he excited her.

Barbara crawled across to him, every movement provoking new feelings in her burning buttocks, her sex so wet she could feel her juices running down her thighs into the tops of her stockings. She opened her mouth and took his cock between her lips, using her tongue to caress the whole length of it. The hardness and heat of it caused new feelings to tremble through her sex as she imagined what it would feel like thrusting into her. She wanted to show him that she could be a good lover, that she could give him pleasure as great as he had given her. She eased her mouth right down on him, swallowing him completely, then pulled up again and sucked his glans.

'Not very impressive.'

She tried harder, forcing him into the back of her throat until she almost gagged, then using her tongue to circle his shaft. The feeling of his cock buried in her mouth made her sex pulse with desire, reviving the orgasm she had just experienced.

Pulling her mouth off his cock she sucked down the tube of his urethra until she reached his balls, then gobbled them both into her mouth.

She felt his cock pulse strongly and moved her lips up to take it deep in her mouth again. She wished she could have used her hands, fingered his balls. She moved her head up and down, trying to use her tongue to increase the pressure as he slid in and out of her. She could feel he was coming but just as she thought he was going to spunk he took his cock in his hand and pulled out of her.

'You're useless,' he said. He pushed her away and got to his feet, picking up his clothes. 'I'm late for dinner.'

She watched as he stepped into black briefs and trousers.

'What about me?' she said forlornly.

'What about you?'

'Aren't... aren't you going to fuck me?'

He laughed.

'I thought I'd given you want you wanted.'

'I want to be fucked,' she said.

'Get up,' he said in that authoritative tone she had first heard at the party.

She managed to struggle to her feet. Casually he wrapped an arm around her waist. He guided her over to the bedside table where he stooped and took a large black dildo from the drawer. He slipped it between her legs, pushing it into her wet sex and turning it on.

She gasped. Part of her wanted to open her legs, let the dildo fall out and show Jack she did not need his humiliating treatment. But that was not the part governing her actions, and instead she pressed her legs together, forcing the dildo deeper and putting more pressure on her clit.

Jack's hand slid down to her buttocks, caressing the weals he had created with the whip. The feeling was indescribable; sensations of pain and pleasure renewed almost as strongly as before. She found herself trembling. She pressed herself against his body, wanting to feel him, hoping against hope he would fuck her but knowing he would not.

'Please...' she whispered, but it was too late. Her orgasm overtook her and she shuddered to a climax, unable to use her hands to cling to him, as she wanted desperately to do.

'You see,' he said quietly. 'It's not about what you want, it's about what I want. That's your lesson for today, Barbara. I hope you've learn it well.'

Chapter Four

'Bring her over here.'

Celine led me forward on the leash. I had been released from the post and she had taken off the blindfold and gag, and the wires attached to my nipple rings, but left my wrists and elbows clipped firmly behind my back. A leather hood had been pulled over my head. It had holes for my eyes and mouth and was laced tightly at the back so the leather moulded to my face.

I estimated I had been left on the T-shaped post for over an hour before they released me. With the wires from my new nipple rings pulled taut even the slightest movement made me tremble with a sexual tension that kept me on the brink of orgasm. My nipples were throbbing constantly, an intoxicating mixture of pleasure laced with pain. If I had twisted my shoulders slightly to pull on the wires I could easily have brought myself off, and it was a difficult temptation to resist. But I didn't want to give myself away in case I was meant to be passive, as a result of whatever they were supposed to have done to me.

Madam Celine led me through an old house that had been meticulously restored, the pale carpets thick and the walls of panelled wood.

There was a mirror on the wall. I looked at the strange sight of myself as I walked passed, the nipple rings catching the light, my face hidden by the black leather helmet.

We had entered a small study, its walls lined with books. Sitting behind a desk was a woman I recognised at once - it was the brunette. She even had her hair in the same style, swept up into a chignon to reveal her sculptured neck. She was wearing a pair of skin-tight black leather trousers and a matching sleeveless leather top with a plunging neckline. It revealed a great deal of the lacy black bra that supported her large breasts. The woman was looking at a clipboard.

'All right, you may leave us.'

Celine immediately turned and left the room, closing the door behind her.

'What do you think of your piercings? Pretty, aren't they? Are you grateful?'

I said nothing. The truth was that I'd long-since wondered what it would be like to have my nipples pierced. I'd told Jack that, on the fateful night Tony found us together. And Tony had overheard.

'Answer me.'

'Yes.'

'You will call me Madam M when you speak to me. Assume the first position.'

I remembered that was what Celine had called lying prone on the floor. If I was to continue to pretend to be under the woman's spell I had to obey all orders without question. I slipped to my knees, rolled onto my side then slid onto my front. Immediately my nipples touch the carpet I gasped with pain.

'A little tender I expect,' Madam M said. I heard her get to her feet. 'But then pain turns you on, doesn't it?'

I didn't know what to say. My throbbing clit was certainly testimony to my excitement but I wasn't sure whether it was the pain or everything else that was happening to me.

'Answer me,' she snapped, 'or I'll have your clit pierced too.'

'Yes.'

'Roll over onto your back.'

I did so willingly, happy to relieve the pressure on my nipples. Madam M straddled my head and I found myself gazing up her long legs to the leather stretched over her crotch. She raised a foot and placed a metal heel on my left nipple.

I gasped. My body was seized with shudders of pain but at the same time I could feel my clit pulsing.

'You see,' she said. 'That's what pain does to you. You must learn that lesson.'

She removed her heel then stooped down. I saw she had a thick gold chain in her hand. It had little clips at each end which she attached to the rings in my nipples. I was fearful she was going to pull it, but instead she squatted down on her haunches right over my face so her crotch was no more than an inch from my nose.

'Lick,' she ordered.

I strained upward and licked the smooth leather.

'Harder.'

I pushed my tongue hard against her, but I had to strain up to reach and with my arms behind my back the pressure on my neck muscles was enormous. After a minute or so I could stand it no longer and had to rest my head back on the floor.

'You're useless,' she said, getting to her feet. 'Stand up.'

Even this simple operation was not an easy task. I had to roll onto my side and then try to lever myself to my knees before I could stand upright. But the only way I could get up was by crawling over to the wall and using it to support myself as I struggled to my feet. All the time Madam M watched me with an expression of contempt, as if I had failed her again.

'Are you a lesbian?'

'I don't know. I can't remember anything.'

'When Madam Angel sucked your pussy you had an orgasm, isn't that true?'

'Yes. I don't... I don't...' I couldn't think what to say without betraying myself. If I told her I knew I was bisexual that would give the game away.

'All right, we have to give you a name.' She smiled, her lips parting to reveal perfectly structured white teeth. 'Perhaps we should call you useless. What do you think?'

'I have a name,' I said.

'Oh do you? What is it then?'

'I can't remember.'

'You have nothing, you are nothing. I am going to name you. Natalie. Yes, Nat. That will remind us all that you're like an irritating little fly that we can swat any time we like. Do you like it?'

'No.'

'Address me as Madam M or I will have you taken back to the treatment room and have you strung up by your nipple rings.'

She picked up a marker pen from the desk and used it to write the word NAT on my stomach.

'Now listen to me, and listen very carefully.'

As she said the words I felt a sense of wellbeing flooding over me. I suddenly felt terribly tired and couldn't keep my eyes open. I remembered I had heard the words before, that night with Tony. It was obviously the beginning of the process of hypnosis. I struggled to keep awake. Whatever happened I must not let her hypnotise me. I thought of Jack. I remembered how he had whipped me. I tried to think of those strokes of leather burning into my bum.

'You are here to be trained for your master. You belong to him now. You are his slave. You only exist to serve him. You are not a person. You are an object, a possession. You have no will of your own. You name is Natalie M. Repeat it.'

'Natalie M,' I mumbled.

A thick black fog was closing in around me. It was warm and comforting. I desperately wanted to sleep, but I knew I must not.

The door opened and Celine entered.

'I've put her under again. Take her back to the cell. We can start the training tomorrow.'

'Yes, Madam M.'

It had been a week. One hundred and sixty eight hours since she'd seen Jack. She had practically counted each one of them. She couldn't sleep. She wasn't hungry. She was exhausted not only through lack of rest but by the fact that it was impossible for her to sit or lie down without thinking about sex, without thinking about Jack and having to seek relief, however temporary, with her own hand or vibrator. Some days she masturbated six or seven times. She'd masturbated in the shower, on the kitchen table, and in bed. She done it naked and fully dressed with her skirt around her waist and her panties pulled to one side, the urge too urgent to spend time pulling them off. She'd done it dressed up in stockings, high heels and a tight corset while she stood in front of the mirror imagining Jack watching her.

She could remember every minute in his flat. She remembered how he had whipped her while she knelt on the floor, how every stroke had provoked pain that twisted into extraordinary pleasure. She remembered how his cock felt in her mouth and her disappointment when he pulled out before he'd come and how he casually thrust the dildo into her and stood beside her while she orgasmed, completely unable to control herself. Every second played in her head as she masturbated.

He'd said he would call her and not to call him. She'd almost given up hope when finally he phoned her mobile. He told her to come to his flat at seven. He hadn't given her any alternative and hung up before she'd even had a chance to tell him she'd be there.

She got a taxi to Kensington High Street. As she walked towards Melbury Road her heart was starting to beat faster again. She remembered Jack had told her at the party that he had a unique talent when it came to women, and there was no doubt in her mind that he had tapped into some profound unconscious impulses in her psyche. What was most surprising was that she'd had no idea they were there. It was true she'd had vague fantasies about being submissive, but she had never been able to be specific about them, had never pictured herself in a scenario of master and slave.

She knew she should not be pursuing their affair, but she was completely unable to think rationally when it came to him. She supposed in the end her husband was to blame. In the last few years she had the impression that all Tony cared about was making money, and she had become a trophy wife, someone to be seen with at parties, a status symbol like his car. Tony's real needs were expressed in his desire to make money, not in the bedroom.

It might be her fault too, of course. When their sex-life had started to wane she did all sorts of things to tempt him. She'd gone to his office in the middle of the day wearing nothing but stockings under her coat. She'd let him discover her in bed with a dildo. She'd crawled under the table in the dining room and given him a blowjob before he'd finished his meal. But the truth was none of these things had really led to the sort of sex they'd had in the beginning. She provoked him to fuck her certainly, but he'd shown little or no interest in making sure she was satisfied too.

She buzzed the entry-phone on the ground floor and the door opened almost at once. She walked through into the spacious, rather old-fashioned foyer, the dark red carpet more than a little threadbare from continual use.

She rode up in a clanging old caged lift feeling a wave of sexual urgency flooding through her. His flat was right opposite the lift doors. She rang the doorbell.

'On time,' he said as he opened the door. He wore slacks and shirt but no shoes or socks.

He ushered her in.

'Next time you come I want you to take your clothes off in here.' He indicated a door to the right. 'Not your pretty lingerie of course. That would be a waste.'

'All right,' she said. Inwardly she was trying to hide her excitement at the fact he had clearly thought about seeing her again.

'I want to show you something,' he said.

She followed him down the hall.

'In here.'

She stood in the open doorway. The room had no window, with black walls and a black carpet with a substantial beam running across the middle of the black ceiling. Hanging from the beam were various leather harnesses, ropes, chains and pulleys. There were metal rings attached to the wall and an odd piece of furniture which could just about be called a chair. Against one wall was a double bed with leather cuffs and chains attached to each corner, the mattress covered with slick black rubber.

'This is where I like to play games,' he said. 'Now take your dress off.'

She had spent a great deal of money on new lingerie, and was wearing a black satin waspie which cinched in her waist and left her breasts bare. It had suspenders holding pearl-coloured stockings with a contrasting black heel and seam. She was not wearing panties.

'How pretty you look,' he said in the mocking tone he often adopted with her. 'But next time I want you to wear panties.'

'I thought...'

He stood behind her and cupped her breasts. Her nipples were hard.

'Sit in the chair,' he said. She could feel the heat of his cock and pressed back against it.

'Why don't you just fuck me?' she said.

'Because that's not what you want.'

She turned and looked at the 'chair'. It consisted of a wide board set back at an angle. Sticking out from the board at waist level was a padded V-shaped projection covered in black leather.

The only way she could sit in the chair was to perch herself on the part of it where the projections joined the sloping back, then spread her legs apart and rest them on the two limbs of the V-shape. The projections left her legs dangling from the knee, which meant she was sitting with most of her bottom unsupported and her sex exposed, which was clearly the purpose of the construction.

'Comfortable?'

The chair was furnished with leather straps. He wrapped them around the top of her thighs, just above her knees, around her waist and above her breasts. He pulled her wrists behind her where leather cuffs attached to the back of the chair held them. Finally he wrapped leather cuffs around both her ankles and pulled them back under the seat and clipped them to it. He had rendered her completely powerless. The only part of her body she could move was her head.

'What are you going to do to me?' she asked.

He stood between her legs, his erection tenting his trousers.

'Whatever I want.'

He leant down and kissed her, but as she pushed her tongue out he pulled back.

'Whatever I want,' he repeated.

A hand caressed her throat and then slid down to her breasts, moving across the upper slopes. He took her right nipple between thumb and forefinger and pinched, making her moan. He stroked it slowly then worked his way down across the satin of her waspie to her tummy. A finger slid between her labia. She was soaking wet. She saw a smug smile on his face. He knew what he did to her.

His finger found her clit. She gasped.

'Very needy,' he said, then took his finger away.

He pulled his clothes off and dropped them on the bed. She stared at his cock, a drop of liquid forming at the eye of the circumcised glans.

'Fuck me,' she said, pleading with her eyes.

'That's not exactly what I had in mind,' he replied. He bent his knees and pushed forward until the tip of his cock was parting her labia. It butted up against her clit and she gasped. She tried to strain herself onto it but her bondage allowed minimal movement.

He pulled away, smiling. He turned his back, then moved behind the chair with a leather blindfold in his hand.

'This helps to concentrate the senses,' he said, slipping it over her eyes.

'Please just fuck me,' she said.

'And a gag too.'

'No.'

'Oh yes, a nice penis-shaped gag so your mouth is full of cock.'

He produced a pad, attached to which was a rubber cock. 'Open wide.'

He pushed the dildo into her mouth and strapped it tightly in place. It reached to the back of her throat and was uncomfortable. She was dependent on her hearing to guess what he was going to do next.

There was a swish of air and a sting erupted across her breasts. She gasped into the gag. She tensed. A scorching line exploded across her breasts again, this time hitting her nipple as well.

He alternated the strokes. The pain was intense. Her breasts were on fire, but as the last stroke bit she knew she was going to come. She knew he was watching her, and that was enough to tip her over the edge and plunge her into a full on climax, her screams of pleasure muffled on the rubber penis that filled her mouth.

As she recovered her senses she thought she could feel the heat of his cock near her sex. His fingers were playing with her tortured nipples. She felt his breath on her breasts and then his mouth took over; biting, sucking, licking. Her nipples throbbed with pleasure and with pain as Jack alternated between biting and sucking. Waves of pleasure were mounting again.

She put her head back and screamed, the sound muffled by the penis gag, and before the waves of bliss had begun to die down his cock was plunging deep into her vagina. There was no resistance. Her sex was open and wet. He thrust deep. The position of the chair and the way she was tied to it meant his penetration was profound. Her sex clenched around him. His thrusts were so powerful they pulled her legs and arms against the bonds that held her, their rhythmic creaking intensifying her excitement.

Jack had stamina. It seemed to go on and on. But eventually, as her cunt clenched around the pistoning rod of flesh that impaled her, she knew he was going to come too. She wished she could hold him and hug him tight, but she couldn't, so she concentrated on using her sex to milk him, and was rewarded with a violent spasm, followed by another. She heard him grunt and then felt a hot, silky wetness flooding her.

'You see,' he panted in her ear, 'I'll always give you what you want.'

Chapter Five

I woke up when the light came on. I was feeling warm and contented. Though there was no natural light in the room and I hadn't the faintest idea what time it was I instinctively felt it was morning and that I'd had a good night's sleep, despite the bonds that anchored my wrists and ankles to the metal frame of the bed.

For a moment I realised I couldn't remember my name. The word Nat kept going over and over in my head. Nat. Nat. Natalie. Was that my name? I concentrated. My memory seemed to have gone. I could remember everything that happened yesterday up until the time I'd been taken into Madam M's office. Then there was another blank. I knew that was a problem but I couldn't remember why. What was happening to me?

Suddenly another name floated into my head. Barbara. Yes, Barbara. I was Barbara. The name brought everything flooding back; my husband, my affair, all the things that had happened. I also remembered being taken into Madam M's office and recognising her as the mysterious and beautiful brunette who seemed to have dominated my thoughts since I'd arrived in these strange premises. But what I couldn't remember was how I'd come to be lying chained to the bed. How I'd got from Madam M's office to the cell was a complete blank. And the most worrying thing of all was that I'd had trouble remembering who I was and my past. The treatment Madam Celine had mentioned was clearly intended to wipe my memory and had not succeeded. I'd assumed that treatment was over but it was obvious that whatever they were doing was continuing. I'd read about sleep therapies and wondered if they had done something to me while I slept. I knew one thing for sure; I mustn't go under. It had taken me some time to reinstate my memory this morning, and if the treatments continued that would only get worse. I must find a way to resist whatever they were doing.

My body was not as severely restrained as it had been yesterday morning. I looked down my naked body. My nipples looked as tender as they felt, linked by the chain between the gold rings that pierced them.

I lay back and stared at the ceiling. Clearly my husband had arranged for me to be brought here to undergo some sort of behavioural therapy, to make me an obedient and submissive wife.

The door opened.

'Good morning.'

I recognised her voice but not her face. I had never seen Madam Celine's features until now because they'd been covered in the rubber helmet. She was beautiful. She had large eyes and a seductive mouth, and her long blonde hair was worn in a ponytail. She wore a red leather halter-top which barely contained her breasts, and a matching miniskirt. Her long legs were sheathed in glossy black nylon and she wore red high-heeled shoes.

She operated a switch by the door. I heard a grinding of electric motors coming from behind me.

Madam Celine leant over me and unbuckled my wrists from the cuffs. Whether deliberately or not she pushed her breasts into my face in the process. She turned around and released my ankles too, giving me a good view of her toned buttocks and the crotch of her black satin panties. I could see the tops of her stockings. I felt my clit throb. Whatever else Jack had done to me, he had certainly liberated my attraction to women.

'Did I give you permission to look up my skirt?' she quizzed.

'No.'

'No, Madam Celine, you idiot.'

She slapped my breast and I yelped.

'Get up,' she ordered.

After lying in bondage for so long this was not an easy feat to accomplish. For the first time in my new existence both my arms and legs were free, but they had been confined for so long they were unwilling to cooperate with the directions I gave them.

Madam Celine took hold of my arm and turned me around. I saw that a panel had opened in the wall behind the bed and inside it was a white-tiled cubicle. She thrust me inside. Immediately the panel slid closed again.

There was a small toilet bowl in one corner. My need was urgent and I used it immediately. The bowl flushed the moment I stood up again. Almost before I had finished a jet of soapy water shot out from nozzles buried in the wall. After a moment or two the water shut off and I was left covered in suds. I scrubbed my body as best I could, carefully avoiding my nipples and the chain attached to them. I washed away the name under my breasts. A second flood of water spurted from the nozzles, washing away the soap. Then hot air blew from the ceiling, drying my body and hair completely.

There was no mirror. Once again I had no opportunity to see myself. I was pretty sure this was intentional. If I'd really had my memory wiped clean, not being able to see myself was a means of ensuring I didn't get a reminder of who I had been before.

The blast of air stopped and the panel slid open again.

'Get out here,' Madam Celine ordered.

I stumbled back into what I had come to think of as my cell. She was standing by the bed where she had placed a curious leather garment. It was a leather corset with shoulder straps, laced at the front but with two tubes of stiff leather, each with a zip running almost in parallel down the back.

'Stand still.'

Madam Celine unclipped the chain that joined my nipple rings together then picked up the garment and wrapped it around my body. The laces were drawn tight, squeezing my waist.

'Your arms are surplus to requirements,' she said as she pulled my left arm behind my back and fitted it into one of the leather tubes. I heard the zip being pulled up, imprisoning my arm tight against my back. The right one followed, forcing my shoulders back and thrusting my breasts out.

The corset had two holes that revealed my nipples. Madam Celine took hold of the nipple rings and clipped the chain back in place. I gasped, my nipples still sore.

'Now eat,' she said.

Two bowls had been placed on the floor by the door. I was incredibly hungry. I got to my knees and crawled over to them. I ate hungrily, trying to ignore the humiliation of what I was doing. I drank some of the water.

'Over here,' Madam Celine said. 'Watching a girl behaving like a dog has always turned me on.'

She was sitting on the bed with her skirt up around her hips. She had pushed the crotch of her panties aside and was fingering her hairless sex, one hand holding her labia open while a finger of the other circled her clit.

'That's all you are, isn't it, Nat M? A bitch.'

'Yes, Madam Celine.' I don't know why but her voice and the words she said thrilled me to the core.

'Come here and serve your mistress, bitch,' she said.

I crawled over to the bed. She hooked a leg over my shoulder and around my back, digging her heel into the leather and forcing my mouth to her sex. I pushed out my tongue, found the little nut of her clit and licked it.

'Harder.' She reinforced her message by kicking her heel into my back.

I pressed her clit and rubbed by tongue against it. I heard her moan and felt her tremble.

'Yes, like that.'

She moaned again and I felt her thighs tighten around my head. She hooked her ankles together and locked her fingers into my hair, pulling my mouth even harder onto her sex. She sighed and I felt juices coating my chin.

For a moment she did nothing, holding me tightly between her thighs and making it hard for me to breathe. My clit and my nipples throbbed in unison. I could smell and taste her juices on my lips. I imagined how it would feel to have her mouth on my sex at the same time, but I knew my orgasm was not on her agenda.

Madam Celine unwound her legs, positioned a foot on my shoulder and pushed. I toppled back onto the floor. With a cruel smile she knelt down, took hold of my ankles and pulled my legs apart, leaning forward until her face was only inches from my sex. She took the nipple chain and lifted so my nipples were stretched up through the holes in the leather corset. The pain was intense but so was the pleasure that came with it. I felt a finger probe between my legs and touch my clit.

'You're soaking wet, you little lesbian bitch. Wouldn't you just love me to lick that pussy of yours?'

'Oh yes, Madam Celine.' I could feel the heat of her breath against my labia. She lowered herself until her lips were touching the yielding lips at the entrance of my vagina. I could not help but moan. I dared to believe she was going to push right down on me and bury her face in my sex.

'Well I'm not going to,' she said, getting to her feet. 'Get up.'

In my tight bondage this was not a simple operation. Without my arms to help me I could not lever myself to my feet and she knew it. She stood over me and watched as I wriggled and writhed to try and get to my knees. It was impossible. Finally she relented and took me by the shoulders to pull me up.

A pair of high heels was placed on the floor and I was made to put them on. Madam Celine buckled the ankle straps. She picked up the leather helmet I had worn before and laced it tightly around my head, but this time did not add a blindfold.

'Open your legs,' she said with a cruel smile.

She took a thin chain. It had two spring-loaded clips at each end, one slightly bigger than the other. She hooked the smaller to the middle of the chain between my nipples, then held the other clip open. Pinching my labia together around my clit she allowed the other clip to sink into my tender flesh.

I squealed with pain. My clit was trapped and squeezed.

'Follow me.' She walked to the door.

Tentatively I walked forward, the clip making each step a new experience in pain and pleasure. It dragged my nipple rings down, so that my nipples too were hurting.

I found myself in a narrow corridor with doors on either side along its length, but no windows. At the end a staircase led up to a door, which opened onto a hallway, with a blue carpet and pale blue walls and oil paintings, mostly abstracts, hung at regular intervals.

Kneeling on the floor was a man wearing a garment similar to mine. His nipples too had been pierced and the rings joined with a chain and, apart from the leather corset, and a helmet like mine, he was naked and busy licking along the skirting board with his tongue. I could see that his buttocks were marked with several crimson stripes, and he flinched as Madam Celine passed by, though she ignored him completely.

I was led into a reception room furnished with comfortable sofas and armchairs. Not only was there another man in a leather corset with pierced nipples and chain, but there were three women too, also identically dressed to me except that they did not have leather helmets and I could see their faces. And unlike me their nipples were not pierced, though they were wearing nipple clips joined by a chain and a chain ran down to a clip pinching their sex lips.

I saw Madam Angel in the shiny rubber she had worn on the first day, and there were two other women I'd not seen before, dressed in the same way as her.

Sitting down chatting amiably to each other were four other people, two men and two women. The women wore elegant cocktail dresses and the men dinner jackets with crisp white shirts and black bowties. All were drinking champagne from crystal flutes. What I had already begun to think of as the 'slaves' were serving these guests. Two of the girls and the man had little trays hooked around their necks and were carrying plates of tiny canapés, carefully circling the room with them. The third female slave knelt with her forehead pressed to the carpet at the side of one of the suited men, her buttocks raised so he could use his fingers to play idly with her sex lips.

Clearly I had been completely wrong about the time. It was evening, not morning as I'd thought.

I saw the guests examining me closely as Madam Celine pulled me over to them.

'She's new,' one of the women said. She raised a hand to my nipple chain, pulling it until my nipples were stretched and the clip on my clit bit even more deeply. I gasped. 'Oh, such a sensitive little thing,' she said in a mocking tone.

Another door opened and Madam M strode into the room. She looked magnificent. She was wearing a hugging strapless dress of yellow, which clung to her body so tightly it was obvious she was not wearing any underwear, other than almost transparent tights.

Behind her was a man. He was wearing a white dinner jacket with a black bowtie. It was Tony.

'Take the clip off,' Madam M ordered.

Celine moved to obey. She reached between my thighs and opened the clip on my clitoris. I almost collapsed under the shock of pain as the blood rushed back into the tiny knot of nerves. I gasped, as Celine's hand held my shoulder to steady me, and as I'd come to expect the wave of pain was followed by an intense wave of pleasure.

'First position,' Celine barked, prodding me in the back.

I struggled to obey. I didn't want to give any clue that I was not as obedient as they thought I was, so I slipped to my knees and rolled onto my side. I straightened my legs and turned onto my front.

'I thought you'd like to see her before we have dinner,' Madam M said to my husband. I saw her red satin shoes in front of my face. 'Kiss them,' she said.

I willingly pressed my lips to the satin. Buried somewhere in my psyche was a very clear desire to obey her commands.

'Most impressive. And you've achieved this in one day?'

'Yes. She'll go into proper training tomorrow, as we discussed. Stand up, Natalie.'

I rolled onto my back, but had to have support from Celine before I could get to my feet. I could smell the familiar scent of Tony's aftershave.

'And you were right about her. The more she's disciplined the more excited she becomes. It makes her terribly easy to control.'

'The nipple rings look very sexy.'

'Yes, and so practical. She can be effectively bound to whatever you choose whenever you choose.'

'What about the helmet?'

'We keep it on at all times. She is not allowed to see her face in the mirror for the first two weeks. It reinforces the idea that she is anonymous, without a face or a personality.'

'How clever. I've never seen her so excited,' he said. He touched my breasts then pinched around the rings. Despite the pain I was determined not to make any sound this time.

'I don't want you making any reference to the past,' Madame M chided him. 'You understand. Her life began here. That is important.'

'Yes, sorry.'

'It's a precaution to make sure the conditioning works.'

'Anything else I should remember?'

'No, you shouldn't have any problems. Bill had to go out tonight so she's agreed you can borrow Angela after dinner. I think you'll find it very interesting. She's just finished her training so she'll help you in any way you want.' Madam M turned to the rest of the guests. 'Well, ladies and gentlemen, shall we go and eat?'

They all nodded and Madam M led the way through the door by which she'd entered.

Tony patted my cheek proprietarily. 'Goodbye, Nat,' he said, before he turned to follow them.

For a moment I was tempted to blow my cover and tell him what I thought of him and this place in no uncertain terms. But there were two things stopping me. Firstly I wanted to know exactly what he had in mind for me, how he imagined he could get away with it. And secondly, the sexual arousal I felt since being brought to the strange house was so strong, and so pervasive that, for the moment at least, I didn't want it to end.

Madam Celine led me out of the room. We turned into a spacious lobby and walked up a curving staircase to the first floor. I was taken along a landing, where Madam Celine opened a door at the end and ushered me inside.

I found myself in a luxurious bedroom with heavy drapes, a huge double bed and a cream carpet. It had the aroma of expensive perfume. The walls were decorated in cream silk and there were two oil paintings lit by brass lamps, both depicting acts of sex, one with a man about to insert his cock into the exaggerated sex of his partner, and the other where the same woman had her lips poised at the glans of an equally oversized penis, which she was holding in both hands.

Standing in the room was another female slave. She was dressed in a black lace basque with a frilly hem and a quarter-cup bra which pushed her naked breasts upwards. She wore black stockings attached to the suspenders of the basque, but no panties, her sex shaved. Like me her nipples were pierced but they were not chained together. Like me also her arms were strapped behind her back, but by leather cuffs at her wrists and elbows. She had large green eyes, smooth lips and, like me, red hair which fell in soft waves to her shoulders. A metal bar had been placed between her legs, attached to two leather cuffs which were strapped around her ankles.

Madam Celine unclipped the chain from my nipple rings. 'Stay where you are,' she ordered.

She walked across the room and opened a walnut armoire. She returned with a metal bar like the one the other woman had bound between her ankles. Forcing my legs apart she strapped it in place. She went to the bedside table. She opened it and took out two short chains with the familiar spring-loaded clips at each end. She clipped them to our rings, so our nipples were just a couple of inches apart.

Without a word she gathered up the redundant chains and walked out of the door.

'What's your name?' I asked.

'Angela M. Keep your voice down. Don't you know anything?' It was obvious she thought the room was bugged in some way.

My arms, my shoulders and my legs ached but it did not diminish my excitement, and clearly she felt the same. I closed my eyes, and subconsciously began to roll my hips and push against her.

'That's nice,' she whispered. She responded by gently twisting her shoulders so the rings on her nipples nudged against mine. There was a slight noise and sharp pulse of pleasure. I gasped.

'You have to be quiet.'

'Sorry,' I whispered.

She pushed forward until our breasts were squashed together. Then she pulled back until the chains were taut and our nipples stretched. She did this four or five times until we were both gasping with pleasure and my clit was pulsing.

'Use my thigh,' she whispered in my ear. She shuffled around awkwardly, the nipple chains stretched to the maximum, until she was pressing her thigh against my sex, the two metal bars at our ankles strained to the limit.

'That's so lovely,' I moaned.

'Be quiet.'

I concentrated on rubbing my sex lips up and down her thigh. I felt them open to expose my clit. It was still sore but ultra-sensitive, and caressing against Angela's silky skin, occasionally catching the hard nub of a suspender that held her stockings taut, created a wonderful sensation.

'You'll make me come,' I whispered.

'Only if you can do it without a noise,' she said.

Clamping my mouth shut I rubbed harder. My excitement increased. This was the first time since I'd found myself in the house that I had the freedom to make myself come, if *freedom* was the right word when my body was in such tight bondage. But as I rubbed my clit against the hot flesh I knew it was not enough. I needed something more. It was shocking but I needed to feel the intensity of pain. She seemed to sense it too. She eased back so the chains pulled my nipples taut, and I gasped as the metal stretched my tender flesh. The stab of pain transferred itself to my sex and in seconds I was coming, rubbing against her smooth flesh.

I recovered from my orgasm and moved around, trying to return the compliment, pushing my thigh between Angela's legs, but she pulled back.

'No,' she whispered. 'I make too much noise when I come, I can't stop myself.'

'Are you waiting for me?'

I could not see who had entered the room, but it was Tony. I felt his hand running down my back. When it reached my buttocks he pinched and I couldn't help yelping.

'Sensitive little thing, aren't you?'

I said nothing. I was determined not to reveal the truth.

'Reply when I talk to you.' The rebuke was accompanied by a stinging blow to my left buttock.

'Yes.'

'You're going to be trained to call me master. So you might as well start now.'

'Yes, master,' I intoned. Despite the circumstances the word excited me. It was the word of a slave, an object, helplessly bound with no power to resist anything he might want to do to me, and I found that incredibly exciting.

'That's better. You've got a lot to learn about how to treat a man properly.'

He walked around us. He had taken off his jacket and bowtie and was unbuttoning his shirt. He pulled off his shoes and socks and I heard a zipper as his trousers and black briefs followed. His cock was already beginning to grow.

He rounded on Angela, pushing into her back, his hands squeezing between us to cup her breasts. It was the first time I'd seen my husband touch another woman. She groaned as his hands squeezed. I could imagine that cock crushed against her buttocks.

'Would you like me to fuck you, Angela?'

'I would love it, master, if that's your pleasure.'

He laughed. 'You see, Nat. The perfect answer. What matters here is what I want. That's all that matters. Do you get it?'

I did not reply.

'Answer me. You've just earned your first punishment.'

36

'Yes, master.' It was extraordinary but Tony was treating me just as Jack had, like his slave.

He unclipped the chains from Angela's nipples, leaving them hanging loosely from mine, then stooped and released her ankles from the cuffs.

'Step back,' he ordered.

She stepped away from me.

'Now before we proceed there's the small matter of punishment for your insolence, isn't there Nat?'

'Yes, master,' I said.

'You do need to be punished, don't you, Nat?'

'Yes, master.'

'Good. You see Madam M was right about you. You are a good subject.'

He circled me, examining my body as if he hadn't seen it before, flicking at the chains hanging from my nipples.

'Do you know, the idea of whipping you is turning me on? I'd never have guessed it, but I'm really into all this. It's like a part of me I've only discovered since meeting Madam M. So I suppose you've done me a favour.'

I understood exactly what he meant. How odd that it had taken my affair with Jack to reveal how we both felt.

He pulled me forward. I almost fell because of the spreader bar, but I managed to keep my feet as he guided me to the bed.

'Rest your forehead on the bed.'

I bent forward and did so. I felt his hand caressing my upturned buttocks.

'Angela, get me a cane.'

From my upside down view I saw her go to a china umbrella stand. But instead of umbrellas there were a number of canes. She selected one with her mouth and brought it back to the master. He took it from her lips.

'What a clever mouth you have. We'll put that to good use later.'

He swished the cane through the air. I saw him taking up position behind me. Despite fear I felt a tingle of anticipation in my buttocks.

Thwack! The cane cut down across my bottom, my flesh compressed under the impact. I felt a lurch of pain and struggled instinctively against my bonds, desperate to free my arms to protect myself.

'Not bad for a beginner,' he said, almost to himself.

Thwack! Another cut of the cane seared across my buttocks, just higher than the first. The pain quivered through my body.

Thwack! Thwack! I was unable to stop tears welling in my eyes, but that didn't mean my body wasn't converting the searing pain into equally intense pleasure.

Thwack! Thwack! I could barely stand. My knees threatened to buckle, then he struck on the back of them and I slumped to the floor.

Tony threw the cane down. Through tears I saw him climb on the bed and lay on his back, his erect cock in front of me.

'Now let's see what that mouth of yours can do, Angela,' he said, his voice heavy with passion.

Angela got on the bed between his legs, and I watched as she moved her mouth down over his cock.

Tony moaned as she sucked. 'What a clever girl.'

He pushed her off, then moved until his cock was inches from my face and I could see the wetness of Angela's saliva all over it.

'Wouldn't you love to be fucked now, Nat? Wouldn't you love to feel my cock sliding into you?'

'Yes, master,' I said, despite myself. I knew it would not happen. For Tony, making me watch him being fellated by another woman was part of my punishment for having an affair. He thought I didn't know who he was. He could congratulate himself on having humiliated me, on rubbing my nose in my infidelity, knowing I would never be aware of what had happened, and never be able to reproach him for it. And that was clearly what Madam M offered; the opportunity for the wronged party to reap a sweet revenge.

Casually Tony pushed Angela over onto her back, rolled on top of her and centred his cock between her thighs. He took it in hand and used the glans, wet from her mouth, to stroke her clit. She moaned and shivered. He twisted down and fed one of her nipples into his mouth. He bared his teeth and I saw them grip the gold ring that pierced her flesh, and pull.

'Oh, yesss...' Angela moaned. My own nipples immediately spasmed in sympathy.

He did the same to her other breast while he continued to stroke his cock between her sex lips. He was teasing himself, resisting the temptation to plunge into that hot wet vagina and take the ultimate pleasure.

But he couldn't resist. I saw his hand position his cock at the mouth of her vagina. I remembered how Jack had done the same thing to Sandra while I, like now, was bound helpless and made to watch.

'Yesss,' Angela squealed as he plunged into her, stabbing his cock into her until it disappeared completely. I felt my clit tremble in sympathy. Despite my anger at what he was doing to me, how I wished I could feel what Angela was feeling; a rigid sword of flesh buried in the tight sheath of my sex.

Her eyes were closed and she rolled her head from side to side in obvious ecstasy. As her orgasm subsided he began pulling himself out until I could see the wet head of his penis, then plunging in again, his buttocks knotted with tension. She shrieked on each inward stroke, demonstrating what she had told me about her inability to remain silent during sex.

I wanted to turn away. I wanted to do anything but watch him doing things to her that he had neglected to do to me. Yet at the same time I wanted to see everything, every little detail.

His rhythm changed and he began to limit the amount he pulled out, instead circling his hips. I could see his orgasm approaching. I saw the muscles in his thighs tense and his rhythm slow some more. He thrust one last time, his body arched like a bow, then let out a low guttural expulsion of air. She came again too as his spunk erupted, and she screamed even louder.

Eventually he opened his eyes and climbed off Angela. He looked straight into my eyes. There was satisfaction written into his face, the expression of someone who was enjoying their revenge. Even when we first met he never fucked me with as much intensity. He was playing to his audience and to himself.

'Did you enjoy watching us?' he goaded, circling the glistening cock with his hand and wanking lazily.

'Yes, master,' I lied, keen not to earn another punishment.

'But now I think it's time for you to give me a show.'

He climbed off the bed and lifted me onto it, then rolled me over so I was lying on my back, my arms pinned beneath me.

'Kiss her,' he ordered, looking at Angela.

She crawled over then leant and kissed me on the mouth. I felt her tongue pushing between my lips and sucked it hungrily.

'Now sit on her face,' he ordered.

Angela straddled my shoulders. I looked up into her sex. It was glistening with her juices and his viscous spunk. I strained up and kissed her. Spunk dribbled into my mouth and I swallowed it.

Angela eased down on me, allowing me to lower my head back onto the bed. I felt his hands take hold of my ankles again. His fingers played with my sex lips, stroking up and down between them, but then I felt a finger exploring between my buttocks, pushing against my anus, as if to test its resistance. There was little and his finger slid deep inside my bottom, making me groan. Another finger joined it and he explored my rear passage.

His fingers withdrew, and I felt something bigger being pushed against my sphincter. For a moment it resisted, then I felt a hard phallus penetrate beyond the little ring of muscle and push until it stretched my anus. As usual the initial discomfort was followed by pleasure.

'You little slut,' he said.

'Please fuck me, master,' I begged, muffled by Angela's sex.

He pulled her off me and made her lie on her back again. His cock was fully erect. He sat on her breasts so it pulsed above her face. He gripped it and began to wank.

'Lick my balls,' he told her, and she obeyed, and I watched as he shuddered and came. Spunk jetted from the eye of his cock and spattered her face and her hair.

He took my chin in his hand. He raised my head so I was looking straight into his eyes. They were sparkling with a look that was unmistakable. His revenge, for tonight at least, was complete. But what he didn't know was that his plan, for which he had no doubt paid a great deal of money, was not working. I was not an empty vessel ready to be turned into a mindless submissive. I still had all my faculties. I didn't know how I was going to escape, but I was sure I would, and that when I did it would be my turn to savour revenge.

Chapter Six

Her meetings with Jack had become the high spot of her week. She never knew what he had planned for her, which of course only increased her sense of excitement. She knew one thing; he would always have thought up some new way to humiliate or enslave her to his wishes, and the truth was she loved every single minute of it.

The rest of the week was spent reliving whatever he had done to her. Masturbation was no longer an option, it was a necessity in order to relieve the sexual tension that these memories created day and night. She'd even tried to provoke her husband into fucking her, but her efforts had only been rewarded by a few urgent thrusts in the missionary position before he'd ejaculated which, even in her excited state, had failed to bring her any relief.

Jack had created a monster. She had become super-sensitive. Even the act of putting on a bra was capable of tipping her into uncontrollable excitement and her sex was so receptive she relished the feel of her panties rubbing it as she walked. But the elaborate masturbation rituals she had developed for herself, often lying on the bed in some sort of self-bondage, gagged and blindfolded with a vibrator between her bound legs, was nothing compared to the feelings Jack could give her.

He'd given her a key so she could slip into the flat at the appointed time and strip in the cloakroom as he'd insisted. As usual on this visit she had selected her lingerie carefully; a white lace waspie and white hold-up stockings. The waspie had crisscrossed laces at the back, and she struggled to lace it as tightly as she could. It left her breasts bare, but following Jack's preference she wore white lace panties.

The door to the black room was open and Jack was standing in the middle of it. He was naked apart from a pair of briefs.

'You're late,' he said irritably.

'I'm sorry,' she responded, even though it wasn't true.

'Come here and make yourself useful for a change,' he said.

He smiled knowingly. He walked over to the double bed. The mattress was covered with a single violet-coloured sheet. He lay down on it and opened his legs.

'Pull my pants off.'

She did as she was told. She knelt on the bed and took hold of the waistband of his briefs. He lifted his buttocks to help her pull them off. His cock was already beginning to grow.

'Now kneel between my legs,' he said, stretching them apart. 'And put your hands behind your back.'

She did as she was told, her eyes locked on his circumcised cock.

'Lick it,' he ordered. 'You mustn't use your hands.'

She leant forward and touched her tongue against his glans. It reacted, twitching and growing. She licked around the pink flesh and saw it swell again.

'Now suck it.'

Eagerly she sucked his cock into her mouth. She could feel it getting stiffer and harder. She felt her insides churn with excitement. She concentrated on pleasing him, moving her mouth up and down his engorged phallus, teasing it with her tongue, sucking the glans.

'That's enough,' he said suddenly. He sat up. 'I have arranged something special for you tonight. Isn't that kind of me?' He smiled, a cruel smile. 'But first I think you need to be warmed up, don't you?'

Barbara felt a sharp pang of arousal deep in her sex. She knew what this meant.

'I asked you a question,' he snapped as he got to his feet.

'Yes, yes I do.'

'And you do want to be warmed up, don't you Barbara?'

'You know I do.' She was ashamed to say but it was true. She had no idea what part of her psyche had harboured this desire or why. If anyone had told her that being spanked would turn her on she would have laughed in their face. But it did. She could remember in graphic detail that first time at the party, how he had spanked her as she was tied to the tree. She could remember exactly what it had made her feel. She knew there were many reasons she'd wanted to see Jack again, but the fact that he spanked her was perhaps the most imperative.

'Good. Stand up.'

She did as she was told. He examined her body intently.

'Very pretty,' he said.

He had often begun their sessions by spanking her bottom, sometimes with his hand, sometimes with a cane or leather tawse, with her bending over with her legs apart and her hands gripping her ankles, or kneeling with her forehead pressed to the floor and her buttocks raised. She felt a pang of secret pleasure, her buttocks tingling in anticipation. She was glad her husband took little interest in her body, but even so it had been difficult to hide the marks on her buttocks. Fortunately they faded quickly.

But this time Jack had something else in mind. He picked up a pair of leather cuffs.

'Hold your hands out.'

She did as she was told, looking up into his eyes as he strapped the cuffs around her wrists. She couldn't believe the thrill the feeling of bondage gave her. It was a feeling that comes with something forbidden, but delectable. Being helplessly bound also meant she could kid herself that she had no control over the things he did to her.

'Now stand over here,' he said, indicating beneath the wooden beam.

There was a white rope hanging from a pulley above her head. He tied it to the central link on the cuffs, then went over to the wall and pulled on the other end until her arms were stretched above her head, so she could only just support herself on the tips of her toes. He tied the rope to a cleat on the wall.

'Much better,' he said.

He picked up a red ball-gag and pushed it into her mouth, strapping it securely behind her head. It was uncomfortable and forced her lips wide. She felt a stab of fear. He'd never gagged her before when he'd whipped her.

'Don't want the neighbours to hear.' He walked away from her and returned with metal clips, joined by a metal chain.

'Nipple clips,' he said.

She could see that the jaws were serrated, and when a spring-loaded clip bit into her tender flesh the pain was so strong she lost her balance, only her bondage keeping her upright. He applied the second clip.

'It's worse when I take them off,' he told her with a glint in his eyes.

This was a new sort of sensation, a burning pain laced with sexual tension, her breasts sending pulsing messages directly to her clit.

He reached up above his head and took hold of a small length of cord running through another smaller pulley. He tied it to the centre of the nipple chain, then drew the cord taut until the chain was stretched and her breasts were pulled upwards. The pressure made the nipple clips bite deeper and Barbara felt her whole body tremble with pain.

He knelt at her feet and pulled her panties down her legs. Then he took a metal rod with a leather cuff at each end. He spread her legs apart and strapped the cuffs around her ankles so she was unable to close them.

He picked up a leather belt, split in two at one end. She tensed as she saw him raise his arm, and jerked as the first stroke hit her buttocks, the nipple clips pulled taut. He gave her four, her bottom alight. She almost forgot to breathe her excitement was so intense, reduced her to a quivering mass, with no thought of anything but sex.

She looked at Jack, who sat on the bed returning her stare. He was still wearing that cruel smile.

'Hey, she's really pretty.' The voice came from the door behind her. 'Lovely arse.'

A woman walked into the room. She was tall and slender with cropped black hair, and she was naked apart from stockings and a pair of black high-heeled ankle boots. She had a narrow waist and her breasts were large, with nipples the size of strawberries. Her mons was completely shaved.

'Do you like my surprise?' Jack asked.

Barbara shook her head, but in fact she didn't know what she thought. Her first reaction was horror that any woman should see her like this, trussed and almost naked and so clearly aroused. It was quite obvious by the way she was dressed that Jack intended for the three of them to participate in whatever sex game he had in mind, and that unsettled her too. But she also knew on another level that her body did not share her mind's reaction, and that it had lost none of its capacity to respond to Jack's wicked scenarios.

There was no question in her mind, despite her physical reactions, that if she had not been gagged she would have told him to free her. She would have rushed down the hall, dressed and run away. The idea of sharing him, of watching him with another woman, created a feeling of jealousy as strong as any emotion she had felt before. Questions crowded into her mind. How long had he had this other woman, and what did he do with her?

But she was gagged and securely bound and part of her knew she was glad she could not do anything but stand and stare.

'Meet Sandra,' Jack said.

'Hello, sweetie, aren't you just lovely,' Sandra said, her American accent obvious.

She moved behind Barbara and pressed herself against her back. Barbara felt her breasts, soft and smooth against her. The woman ran her hands up to Barbara's breasts. She cupped them, lifting them slightly to relief the pressure from the nipple clips, then dropping them so a new wave of pain made Barbara moan. One hand ran down Barbara's front and fingers touched between her thighs.

'You and I are going to have a good time, aren't we?'

Barbara shook her head. No woman had ever touched her intimately.

'No?' Jack said, mockingly. 'If you don't want it then you'd better go home right now.'

Barbara shook her head again, more vigorously. That was definitely not what she wanted. The idea of putting on her clothes and walking out of Jack's apartment was like a cold shower of reality. She knew precisely why he had said it. He was making her choose, not allowing her to escape the inevitable truth that it was her body and her sexual feelings, not her mind, that was in charge of her actions.

'What, you've changed your mind again? Shall we give her another chance, Sandra? What do you think?'

Sandra ran a finger across Barbara's breast until it touched a nipple clip. 'I love these, don't you? The pain is like sex, isn't it? It makes me cream so much it runs down my leg.'

The finger descended. Barbara tensed as it moved down her stomach to her sex. It settled on her clit. Barbara shuddered. It was not just Sandra's knowing touch that made her react, but the fact that it was another female doing it.

'She's very wet,' Sandra mused.

Barbara saw him smile. He seemed to know exactly how she would react.

'You want more?' Sandra asked, disappearing behind her. Barbara strained to see what she was doing, and saw her pulling a harness up her legs, adjusting it around her waist. Extending from the triangular black leather covering her groin was a large curved dildo. She pressed against Barbara's back again, kissing her neck, then licking up and around her ear.

The dildo moved between her buttocks, between her thighs. It parted the soft labia and probed her vagina. Hands crept around her body, one grasping a breast, the other going back to working on her clit.

43

'Are you going to come for me?' Sandra whispered in her ear.

Barbara felt the dildo being forced into her sex. At the same time Sandra's tongue circled her ear, her finger teased her clit and her hand squeezed her breasts, making the nipple clips bite deeper. Sandra used her hips to push the dildo deep, then made the tip circle in the depths of Barbara's pussy, producing new shocks of sweet bliss.

Barbara was going to come. It was shameful that Jack, once again, should read her so well, that he knew her better than she knew herself. She had no idea she would be so excited by a woman's touch. But he had known.

She looked at his erect cock as the feelings in her sex became too much to ignore, and she came, in Sandra's embrace, being fucked by her from behind.

Dreamily she opened her eyes, her heavy breathing easing.

Jack was lying on the bed, and Sandra was kneeling between his legs, his cock in her mouth. He pushed her away and moved around behind her, gripping her by the hips.

'Yes, yes,' Sandra urged, pushing back against him. 'Fuck me.'

And Jack did. Barbara watched as his cock sank into Sandra's body, and came out glistening with her juices. She saw the girl tremble and her head arch back, stretching the tendons of her throat. She had never done this, never watched another couple fucking.

Sandra's hand slipped between her own legs, and Barbara knew she was frotting her clit. Sandra opened her mouth, moaned, and went rigid. Jack didn't stop fucking her, but looked across at Barbara. Their eyes met. His expression was clear. He was her master and he could do and would do anything he wanted with her, put her through any humiliation or degradation, because he knew that's what she wanted.

Chapter Seven

They led me down the corridor. For once my bondage was comparatively light. My ankles were shackled into leather cuffs and joined by a chain which meant I could only shuffle as I walked, and my hands were cuffed behind my back, but that felt like a degree of freedom compared to the usual bed bondage and leather corset.

I was bathed and dried in the usual manner, then instructed to put on a red rubber catsuit. I had never worn rubber before, and Madam Celine had to demonstrate how to use talcum powder to ease the skin-tight rubber over my body. The catsuit had holes to expose my breasts and sex. The smell and feel of it clinging to my skin was exciting, and my nipples were erect, my vagina moist. A red rubber hood replaced the usual leather one.

I was following Madam Celine. She was dressed in a tight crop-top of black leather, a black leather miniskirt, black tights and black boots. I could not help but enjoy the sensual movement of her hips as she walked. After the treatment

I'd received at Tony's hands I seemed prone to even the slightest provocation, and the idea of pushing my face between her strong thighs and licking the secret female flesh nestling between them was making my clit hard.

I had slept badly. I fought sleep for as long as I could, afraid that Madam M's treatment would somehow gain control and wipe my memory more fully. Eventually I fell asleep and dreamt about Tony. We were at a dinner party where all the other guests were women.

There hadn't been any food, but Tony walked around the table while one woman after another took it in turn to suck his cock, protruding from his trousers. Then we were in an odd sort of concrete room and I was lying on a bed with a naked woman kneeling between my legs and one straddling my face, while Tony stood over me watching. Then the man was not Tony, but Jack.

I woke with a start, afraid that I'd succumbed to whatever they planned for me, but I knew at once that I hadn't because I remembered my name and everything that had happened to me. It was a huge relief.

Madam Celine led me into a room with a wooden floor and white walls, with various pieces of equipment. The walls were hung with metal rings and leather harnesses, clearly intended to bind a victim in various positions.

Some of the equipment was in use. There were six slaves, two men and four women, bound securely into the odd contraptions, while Madam Angel and another overseer I had not seen before patrolled the room, a riding crop in hand, delivering severe rebukes if the slaves were not performing to their satisfaction. The slaves were dressed as I was in rubber catsuits, their intimate bits exposed.

I was led to one of the machines. It looked like a school desk with a bench seat and a sloping top. I was made to slide into the bench and then Madam Celine took a silver chain and ran it through my nipple rings. There was a metal ring attached to the bottom edge of the desktop, the chain threaded through it and padlocked in place.

The object in the middle of the desk looked like a partly inflated balloon.

'Take it in your mouth,' Madam Celine said.

I had no idea what was going on, but leant forward and sucked it into my mouth. It smelt strong. I heard a whining noise and the rubber started to inflate. The whining noise stopped.

'Now squeeze the air out.'

I tried to use my tongue to press against the rubber, but with little success.

'Harder,' Madam Celine ordered. She reinforced her message with a flick of her whip against my upper arm.

I tried to press against the rubber and felt it give slightly. But when I relaxed the pressure for a moment it re-inflated. I realised I needed to use constant pressure to get any results, but it was hard and I couldn't really make any impression on it.

Suddenly the rubber deflated.

'Again,' Madam Celine ordered.

I caught my breath before the rubber swelled up again. This time I managed to press it back a little before it deflated, then re-inflated again.

By the time I had done this three times I was sweating inside the catsuit. My tongue ached and my jaw muscles were getting cramp.

'Again,' was all she said.

Sweat beaded my forehead as I laboured on the rubber balloon. I had little time to watch what the other slaves were doing, but it was difficult not to miss the fact that one of the females was unstrapped from the particular machine she had been exercising on, suspended by her wrist cuffs from chains in the ceiling and given six strokes across her buttocks by the other two mistresses, before being placed back on the machine.

There was little doubt in my mind what would happen if I was deemed to be slacking, but fortunately Madam Celine appeared satisfied.

'You'll do better tomorrow,' she said. She removed the balloon thing from the desk and screwed a lever into a small hole in its place. 'Now use your tongue. Up and down first, then side to side. You are not allowed to use your lips.'

I pushed the lever with my tongue. Like the balloon the resistance was much greater than I'd expected. I managed to push it forward then back again, though I cheated and used my lips a little.

'Do not disobey me,' Madam Celine hissed. She slashed the crop down across the top of my buttocks.

I struggled. With only my tongue I could hardly move the lever at all. Madam Celine was not impressed, but unhooked the chain and pulled me to my feet. I was taken to another piece of equipment. It looked a bit like the crossbar of a bicycle, with a handle at each end. She clipped my nipple chain to the centre of it, then unhooked the clip that joined my cuffs.

'Grip the handles and squeeze,' she said.

I did as I was told.

'Harder,' she snapped.

I was made to squeeze the handles ten times. I don't think I managed to compress the rubber at all, but Madam Celine seemed satisfied with my efforts.

The nipple chain was released and I was made to bend over what looked like a small vaulting horse with a padded top and four legs. My wrist cuffs were chained to rings in the floor just in front of the horse, and my ankle cuffs were attached to its rear legs making it impossible for me to move. Madam Celine inserted a thin metal rod between my lips. At the end of the rod was a metal weight. She told me to hold it, which at first seemed easy but slowly my lips tired and it took more and more effort to keep the rod from falling. After three or four minutes it was impossible to maintain my grip, and the rod slid out and fell to the floor. I was rewarded with another sharp thwack of the whip, before the rod was reinserted.

She moved behind me, and from my upside down view I saw her pick up another rod, again with a metal weight attached at one end. She slowly slid it into my vagina.

'Hold it there,' she ordered.

46

I squeezed my inner muscles, but the rod began to slide out. I squeezed my pussy harder, knowing I would get a stroke of the whip if I failed, but gravity took its toll and the weight fell to the floor. A stinging pain across my buttocks was my reward.

I was made to repeat the exercise ten times, and ten times Madam Celine punished me for what she regarded as failure.

Freeing my cuffs she led me over to where another narrower horse stood. The top was about three inches wide and covered in black PVC, and a stout black rubber phallus projected from the middle. There was a dial on the wall and a lever beside it.

Madam Celine took a small jar from a shelf, poured some lubricant into her palm, then massaged it over the phallus.

'Sit on it,' she said, indicating the slippery implement.

I straddled the horse and felt the phallus nudge between my sex lips. I adjusted by position, then lowered myself onto it. With the lubricant she had applied and the juices the previous exercise had created there was no resistance.

With athletic ease she dropped to her haunches. There were two metal rings in the floor on either side of the horse, and she pulled my ankle cuffs, stretching my legs out to attach the cuffs to the rings. This forced me down even further onto the dildo, and made it impossible for me to lift up.

'Now squeeze,' she said. She operated the lever on the wall beside the machine, and I felt the phallus swelling inside me. Reflexively my internal muscles squeezed. I saw the needle on the dial flicker, and the swelling of the phallus stopped.

'Again,' Madam Celine said.

She made me repeat the exercise twenty times, and the purpose of them was quite clear. They were designed to increase the response of muscles that could be used to please the men who would become our masters. Not only were we being trained to be obedient, we were also to be returned with new sexual skills and abilities.

The rest of the morning was spent in more conventional exercises. I was made to run on the spot and do press-ups and pull-ups, and several other exercises. Any slacking was greeted with further strokes of the riding crop.

By the end I was exhausted and my buttocks were sore. At any time I could have revealed that I knew perfectly well who I was and what they were doing to me. But what would happen then? The chances were I would be taken to Madam M, and this time whatever conditioning she applied would be successful and I would really become the submissive zombie they intended. My only choice at the moment was to go along with what they wanted, while at the same time looking for an opportunity to escape.

After a break when I was returned to my cell for a lunch of stew and bread, Madam Celine arrived to collect me again. She told me to strip off the cuffs and the catsuit. When I was naked the cuffs were buckled on again and she clipped my arms behind my back and my ankle cuffs together with the same short chain. We set off in a different direction and I found myself in a small room decorated in a lush shade of crimson. The only furniture was a square block upholstered in red leather. Fixed to the top of it were four straps, while hanging above it was a metal bar with clips at each end.

'Kneel on that with your knees apart,' Madam Celine ordered.

I did as I was told. She freed my wrists then stretched my arms up above my head and attached the cuffs to either end of the bar. She then folded the leather straps over my legs, one just below my knees and one over my ankles, making it impossible for me to stand up. She then left me on my own, although not for long.

When the door opened again Madam Celine entered with two of the other slaves, a man and a woman. Both wore the same rubber catsuits and helmets I had worn earlier, and I watched as she undid their wrists and ankle cuffs. The female slave had a slender figure with long legs and firm breasts, though their shape was distorted by the holes in the catsuit. Between her legs I caught a glimpse of blonde pubic hair.

The male was shorter. He had an erection, the veins standing out prominently, perhaps because of the tightness of the hole through which it and his balls had been forced.

Madam Celine had a blindfold. She slipped it over my eyes, plunging me into darkness.

'You know what to do,' I heard her say to the couple. 'And you know what will happen if you don't do it well.'

I felt a hand caress my nipple. A tongue wormed into the ring and its soft wetness dallied with the metal, pulling it up and down and making me moan with pleasure. Another hand was running over my buttocks where the collection of marks from my encounter with Tony had been joined by the stinging blows from Madam Celine. It soothed and caressed them. Another hand pushed between my thighs. I felt a warm silky oil being massaged into my sex, while another hand oiled my anus until a finger could penetrate there.

A mouth locked on my sex and a tongue found my clitoris. Another mouth kissed me, a wet tongue forcing its way between my lips.

I could do nothing but give in. Four hands and two mouths caressed and kissed and licked my body, and I swooned with delight. Fingers played with my nipples too, agitating the rings just enough to provoke a delicious mixture of pleasure and discomfort. I moaned. I felt my orgasm blossoming and knew I was going to come.

The clever mouth left my sex and the unmistakable loop at the tip of Madam Celine's riding crop hit my clit a stinging blow. I shuddered under the impact.

'Pleasure and pain, that's what you love, you little slut,' Madam Celine mocked.

It was. Pleasure and pain. I tried to stop trembling. Then the hands and lips were back, and I felt the slave's cock probing between my thighs. It pushed once and slid into me, aided by my shameful juices. I had no idea who he was, but the anonymity actually added to my excitement. As his cock plunged deep into my sex hands caressed my body. The cock fucked me harder and harder. I was on the brink again, but they pulled away and the whip punished my clit for a second time.

'No, please no,' I begged.

'All part of your training,' Madam Celine said.

Again the clever lips and the wily fingers did their work. Warm massage oil was smoothed into my flesh. Hands worked on my breasts, caressing them, my nipples so hard. The rings were pulled, the tender buds pinched and nipped and sucked, fingers pushing into my vagina and arse. I fought my orgasm off, trying desperately to delay the inevitable, but the feelings were just too strong. When the fingers in my sex were replaced by the erect cock I was on the edge of orgasm yet again. But all physical contact withdrew and the cruel whip cracked down on my helplessly exposed clit for a third time.

I was brought to the edge of a climax countless times, and each time my clit was punished, allowing me no relief. Then, finally, I heard the door opening and closing and I was left alone, on the brink, horribly frustrated.

I don't know how long it was before I heard the door open again. A hand removed the blindfold and I blinked.

'I see you've been enjoying your training.' It was Madam M. She stood in front of me wearing a black satin slip that followed every contour of her spectacular body. It had a deep V-neck and I could see her breasts pressed together by a black bra. She was wearing black high heels, and she seemed to tower over me. Her legs were sheathed in glossy black nylon. Her long hair had been pinned up, making her look even more severe.

'Answer me,' she snapped.

'No, Madam M,' I said.

'No? How do you explain this then?' She ran a hand between my pussy lips. I shuddered. My juices coated her fingers.

'I don't know, Madam M,' I said.

'Do you know what turns me on?'

'No, Madam M,' I replied.

'Pain; other people's pain. I'm a born sadist. I get pleasure in seeing other people suffer. Fortunately there are plentiful masochists who can benefit from my predilections. Women like you.'

She produced a thick dildo and a leather harness. She went behind me and knelt on the block, her legs straddling my calves, and pressed against my back, her hands circling my waist. She cupped my breasts, massaging them.

'You are completely helpless. I can do anything I want to you, anything at all, and there is nothing you can do to stop me. There is absolutely no escape. That excites you, doesn't it?'

'Yes, Madam M,' I said. It was true.

Her fingers played with the rings in my nipples. I tensed, expecting her to pull them, my tortured clit pulsing.

'That's why I started this little enterprise,' she said. 'To give myself an endless supply of slaves who I could manipulate for my own satisfaction. Oh, my clients get what they pay for, but in the end that's a bonus.'

She wriggled her belly against my bottom. The silky smoothness of her slip felt deliciously cool against my tortured buttocks, and I could not help but moan with pleasure. A hand snaked between my legs and frotted my clit.

She moved around in front of me. I looked into her eyes. Instead of the disdain and superiority I had seen there before, she was displaying a quite different emotion - lust. Her eyes were sparkling. She picked up the leather harness. It had a triangle of leather at the front, in which was a hole. She fed the dildo through it.

'I'm going to let you fuck me, Natalie,' she said. 'I need it.'

She teased the tip of the dildo between my thighs. It ground against my clit and I gasped. She undid the buckles of the harness and wrapped it around my hips and between my legs, strapping it on tight. I looked down at the dildo sticking out from my groin like a real cock.

I watched as Madam M inched the material of her slip up over her legs and hips, and bunched it around her waist. She wore black silk panties.

There was just enough room on the block for her to slip onto all fours and grind back against the dildo. She reached between her legs to grasp it and guide it, easing aside her panties.

Instinctively I pushed forward, so the dildo slid between the lips of her sex.

She moaned slightly, directing the tip to her clitoris. I moved back and forth so it stroked her little bud and she shuddered. Bound as I was I couldn't move freely, so I held steady as she pushed back and the black rubber sank into her.

Madam's buttocks pressed against my groin and she ground against me, making the dildo twist and its base rub deliciously against my sex. Then she rocked forward and I watched as the dildo emerged, glistening with her juices. She pushed back powerfully again, burying it in herself and making it butt my clit too.

She began a rhythm, slow at first but with increasing speed. Each time she pushed back she uttered a little cry of pleasure and each time I felt the dildo tease my clit. I would have loved to free my hands and wrap them around her, sinking my fingers into those soft breasts, but the cuffs held me firm.

It was a delicious experience, and after my previous frustrations I felt my orgasm nearing. I knew she was coming too, her sobs of pleasure echoing my own. She thrust back and I thrust forward, prolonging and intensifying what we felt together.

After long moments calm descended. Madam M pulled away. For a moment she stayed on all fours in front of me, breathing deeply, and I could see her sex lips and her thighs glistening with juices. Then she got to her feet. She readjusted her panties, wriggled her slip down and walked out, leaving me bound and alone, the harness still strapped around my hips, the dildo still sprouting from my groin.

Chapter Eight

Outside the front door of his apartment block she hesitated. Every time she went to see Jack she was betraying her husband and her marriage. But she told herself it was her husband's fault, that he was neglecting her, that he didn't seem to be interested in sex any more, just his work, so really he only had himself to blame.

That didn't mean she felt any less guilty. But it was not only guilt that made her hesitant. The exquisite pleasures she received at Jack's hands were dark and perverted, and she didn't like to admit to herself that she was capable of relishing such depraved acts. In his 'black room' she was reduced to a sex slave, made to submit without question to anything he wanted, no matter how bizarre or humiliating. The fact that she loved this submission and craved it was what gave her pause. Jack had found a cache of sexual need but wouldn't it be better to turn her back on these atavistic fantasies, to close the door on what lurked beneath the surface of her psyche and gain control of her life again?

She knew the answer was yes. But she knew, just as surely, that she would not let that rational judgement stop her for one moment.

In the lift to his apartment her heart began to beat faster and she felt the breathlessness of excitement seize her lungs. She wondered what he had in mind for her tonight. She never knew. He had never repeated himself. Every visit was a new journey into sexual territory she had never explored before.

She let herself into the apartment at exactly the appointed time, knowing what he would do to her if she were late. She was not expecting him to greet her. The only routine part of the evening was his insistence that she went into the cloakroom and stripped to her lingerie. Tonight she had chosen a lacy blue corset and panties. The corset left her breasts exposed, and it had suspenders that held glossy smoke-coloured nylons.

She opened the cloakroom door. On the toilet seat was a note, *The chains are for you.* She looked around. Hanging from the back of the door were two sets of metal manacles.

She slipped off her outer clothes. She took the manacles from the door. There was a keyhole in each, and a spring-loaded mechanism by which they could be snapped shut.

She wrapped one around her wrist and closed it with a metallic click. Only a few links joined it to the other, so it was a little awkward getting the other cuff on, but she managed it.

The other set were for her ankles. It would be difficult to walk properly with them on, but that was his intention, and it excited her.

She bent and fitted them around her nylon-sheathed ankles and snapped them shut. She managed to shuffle out into the hall, the chains clinking. Feeling the usual cocktail of trepidation and excitement she moved with tiny steps towards the black room, but as she approached she heard Jack's voice from the living room.

'In here.'

The door was ajar and she pushed it open. He was sitting in an armchair with his legs crossed, reading the paper. He did not look up.

'Come over here.' He pointed to a spot on the carpet in front of him.

She shuffled forward, feeling like a pet dog summoned to the side of its master.

'Get on your knees.'

She obeyed at once.

'What do you think of your chains?'

She couldn't think of what to say.

'I asked you a question.'

'I don't know.'

'You don't know? What sort of answer is that? If I want you in chains, if I go to the trouble of buying chains for you, shouldn't you be a little more enthusiastic? Well, Barbara, in future I'm going to keep you in chains quite a lot. It pleases me to see you like this. Is that understood?'

'If that's what you want.'

'I think I've been much too lenient with you.'

He put the paper down and leant forward. He cupped her breasts, one after the other, pinching her erect nipples. He picked up a short strap from the small table next to the chair. He threaded it into one of the chain links between the wrist manacles then pulled them up and buckled the strap around her neck.

'Lie on your back,' he said.

She did as she was told, though it was difficult without the use of her arms.

'So this is her...'

She looked up at a pair of grey corduroy trousers.

'Oh, how rude, I haven't introduced you,' Jack said, getting to his feet. 'This is Tom, a friend of mine. When I told him about you he wanted to see for himself.'

'Jack tells me you like to be submissive,' Tom said. 'Is that true?'

'No.'

'No? Is he lying to me then?'

'No. I mean yes.' She was so confused, so surprised by this turn of events she found answering a simple question a challenge.

'Yes he's lying, or yes you like to be a slave?'

'I like being a slave,' she muttered, feeling herself blush.

Tom walked back out of her field of vision.

'Let's get on with it,' Jack said.

'I've got it here,' Tom replied.

'Tom has bought you a present, Barbara. Isn't that nice of him?'

'What sort of present?' she said weakly.

'It's a dildo. He wants to see you masturbate with it.'

Tom squatted down by her side. She looked at him. He was a thickset man with a broad face, a large nose and piggy eyes. His hair was brown and curly. There was nothing about him she found attractive. He was holding a smooth metal phallus in his hand.

'I can't!'

'Open your legs,' Jack said sternly.

Bemused by what was happening Barbara slid her legs apart as far as the chain would allow. Tom pushed the crotch of her panties aside and slid the dildo between her pussy lips. It was cold and she winced.

'It'll soon warm up, baby,' he said, his voice gruff. He twisted a ring at the base of the dildo and Barbara felt familiar vibrations spreading out into her sex. The two men stared down at her. It was humiliating, to be made to bring herself off in front of a man she had never met before. But as always her body responded with a wave of excitement and her juices flowed.

'Nice tits,' Tom said crudely.

'I think they need a bit of stimulation too,' Jack said.

He produced some nipple clamps and clipped them to her erect buds. She gasped. They bit deep, and turned into a dull ache.

'She loves it,' Tom observed with satisfaction. He unzipped his trousers and extracted his cock, wanking lazily. As she watched he pulled the foreskin back to reveal the bulbous glans.

The feelings in her body were coalescing. The physical stimulation of the dildo and the nipple clips, that unique melange of pain and pleasure, were rushing her to an orgasm, but she knew it was more than that. She knew what was bringing her off so strongly was the extraordinary position in which she found herself, chained and exposed, obeying the whims of a stranger as surely as if she were his slave, as if he owned her and her only role in life was to do as she was told. A part of her didn't want to admit how excited she was, how such humiliating treatment was accelerating her to a climax. But she simply had no choice. She tugged on the chain linking the nipple clamps and the surge of pain pushed her over the edge, making her moan with delight and arch her spine, only her feet, her buttocks and her shoulders in contact with the floor.

As she gradually calmed down her orgasm only left her wanting more. She raised her head. 'Let me suck it,' she begged, eyeing the cock in Tom's fist.

'Good idea,' Jack chuckled. 'Let her suck it for you.'

Tom knelt and leant over her face so she could reach his cock. She sucked it eagerly, circling his glans with her tongue, now so excited she had overcome any qualms about Tom's presence. She managed to cup his balls, caressing them with her fingertips.

From the corner of her eye she saw Jack unzip his trousers and pull out his cock. He moved closer, his cock butting against Tom's. It was too much for her to get into her mouth at the same time, so she moved her lips around and sucked on the side of each, one after the other. She managed to run her tongue under the stout shafts and lick the ridge of each helmet, feeling both jerk as she did. She clamped her thighs around the dildo, wanting to feel the vibrations against her clit.

'That's enough,' Tom said suddenly, pulling away, his cock quivering on the brink of ejaculating. Jack pulled away too.

The two got to their feet. Tom bent over and casually removed the dildo from between her legs, completely unconcerned as to whether she wanted him to or not.

Together they lifted her to her feet.

'Follow us,' Jack ordered brusquely.

In the black room Tom unbuckled the strap from her neck and seized her wrists. He made her bend over a padded stool and used rope to secure the wrist manacles to one of its legs, a few inches above the floor.

'Pull her panties down,' Jack said.

Tom slipped them down to her feet.

Jack held a small key, with which he undid the manacles around her ankles. But her comparative freedom didn't last long, because with two pieces of soft rope he tied her ankles to the stool legs.

He produced a phallus-shaped gag he'd used before, fed it into her mouth and buckled it at the back of her head.

Tom moved behind her, his erection pressing into her buttocks. He ran a hand over the smooth globes, then between her thighs until fingers were resting against her engorged clitoris. She trembled. She felt juices leaking from her. His finger moved between her lips and delved inside. His other hand pulled on the nipple chain, making her moan into the gag.

'She really loves it,' he said.

A blindfold plunged her into darkness. She listened intently. Her body ached, stretched and strained over the stool, but that did not diminish her excitement.

Thwack! Pain flashed across her buttocks like a diagonal line of burning needles. The sound of leather on flesh echoed around the room. Barbara screamed but only a sob got through the gag. The pain turned to bliss, taking her breath away.

She listened intently for any clue when the next stroke was coming, but heard nothing. She braced herself, her muscles rigid.

The whip struck again. Thwack! She gasped into the gag and felt her clit swell.

'Very nice.'

'A perfect cross.'

'X marks the spot.'

Barbara's bottom was on fire, radiating heat. She felt a finger tracing diagonally across her buttocks on the line the whip had left. She could feel that her skin had puckered and raised into a thick welt. The finger was cool and soothing and produced another flood of sensations deep in her core.

She thought she heard the faint rustle of clothes being removed, but couldn't be sure. Hands gripped her hips. An urgent cock nudged her arse. It was slippery and wet, lubricated with something. The hands moved to her buttocks, pulling them apart. She felt the cock nose against her anus. A rush of pure passion washed over her. If she could have screamed out for whoever it was to bugger her she would have, but she only succeeded in letting out a faint moan.

The cock thrust. There was a moment of discomfort as her sphincter resisted, then a shock of pleasure as it relaxed and the slippery phallus sank deep into her rear.

A hand was fumbling at the back of her neck. She felt the strap of the gag loosen and the phallus was torn out of her mouth, and before she had a chance to realise what was coming another phallus, a real one this time, stretched her lips apart and ploughed deep. She swallowed it eagerly, feeling it thrust to the back of her throat.

Her body was trembling with excitement. In her mind's eye she could see herself tied helplessly over the padded stool as the two men thrust into her. The feeling of two hard cocks penetrating her was driving her wild with lust, but she knew her excitement wasn't just physical. Having sex with two men at the same time, two men who treated her like an object merely to be used for their satisfaction, was so outside her experience of normal sex her mind was reeling, every shibboleth, every taboo shattered, every barrier broken. She was allowing herself to be treated like the lowest form of slut and every second of it was exciting her like nothing ever had. She was coming so strongly nothing would stop her.

'The little bitch loves it,' Tom grunted as he buggered her.

'She certainly does.' Jack cupped her cheeks and for a moment caressed them tenderly while he held his cock at the back of her throat. It was the first time he had done anything that resembled affection. She could feel his cock throbbing and thought he was going to come. At the same moment she felt Tom's cock swell in her anus.

'No,' Jack said suddenly, pulling out of her mouth. 'Let's do it properly.'

Tom pulled away too, leaving her draped over the stool, panting. The gag was pushed back into her mouth and her wrists and ankles released. She was pulled up and hustled to the bed. Her orgasm was still throbbing in her veins and her heart was beating rapidly.

'Kneel,' said Jack.

She groped forward until she was kneeling on the mattress. A hand took her manacled wrists and pulled her. She felt a naked body kneeling behind her, a rigid cock prodding her back. Another hand lifted her left knee and pulled it to one side, and she found herself straddling one of the two men. Hands pulled her forward again and she gasped into the gag when she felt her pussy nudge against an erection. The hands took her by the hips and pulled her down onto it. Her vagina was running with juices and she squirmed down, relieved that she could at last do something to satisfy her own needs. She ground her clit against the pubic bone at the base of the man's cock.

Weight moved behind her and a hand stroked her buttocks, something cold and creamy being massaged into her anus. A cock pushed. Fingers dug into her hips. A bulbous globe stretched her sphincter and eased inside.

She came, just as a jet of spunk spattering into the tight tunnel of her anus, and seconds later she heard a groan of pleasure from Tom and felt her vagina filling with hot semen too.

Chapter Nine

Madam Celine was smiling at me. She was watching as I struggled into the clothing she had brought for me. It was a catsuit of black nylon, with long sleeves and a high neck, my breasts visible through the semi-transparent material. It had no crotch and my sex was exposed right round to my buttocks.

When I finished smoothing the nylon over my body I slipped my feet into waiting black stilettoes.

'Very pretty,' Madam Celine said.

I sensed that whatever was going to happen it was not to be part of the usual routine that had been followed day in and day out. I was being prepared for something special, though I was certain I wasn't going to be told what it was. Celine was looking at me with a degree of desire in her eyes, and I wondered if she intended to use me for her own purposes before she took me to my destination. I had the feeling she hesitated, and decided against it.

She picked up two pairs of leather cuffs from the bed and strapped them around my ankles and wrists. Another pair were fitted just above my elbows, my arms held behind my back, elbows almost touching. It forced by shoulders back and my breasts out against the thin catsuit, my nipples already erect.

Finally she pulled a black helmet down over my head. It was made of some sort of elastic material that had the appearance of satin, and had a hole for my mouth and two for my eyes. It had lacing at the back, which she drew tight, my hair pulled through to form a ponytail. It clung to every contour of my face.

She took my arm and led me out along the corridor and into the main house. We climbed the stairs to the first floor and along the corridor where I'd been once before; the night with Tony. She opened one of the bedroom doors and led me inside. It was lavishly decorated with chintz and heavy curtains and a deep cream carpet. The room was dominated by a four-poster bed, modern with square metal posts furnished with small metal rings at regular intervals.

Attached to the two posts at the foot of the bed was a woman. Her ankles and wrists were strapped into cuffs clipped to the metal rings on the posts, so she was standing spread-eagled, facing the bed.

She had long blonde hair and heavy make-up, her eyes lined and shadowed with dark purple. She was wearing a red mini-dress, little more than a tube of skin-tight material with no sleeves. Because of the position of her legs the hem had ridden up over her thighs so it only just covered her panties. Her legs were sheathed in stockings and she wore red high-heels. Around her neck was a thick collar that pushed up under her chin, stiffened leather which made it impossible for her to lower her head. A red ball-gag stretched her lips, and a dribble of saliva had escaped and glistened on her chin.

Celine pulled me over to her. She made me squeeze my way between the bedframe and the woman, facing her. She attached my wrist cuffs to the same metal rings that held the woman's, though she did not secure my legs.

We were left alone.

'Are you all right?' I asked.

The woman nodded.

Remembering what had happened with Angela and my own feelings I slid my thigh between hers. I hoped we might share a few stolen moments of tender sexual relief.

'We can help each other,' I whispered. 'I'm sure you feel the same as me.' I pushed my thigh up against her panties.

She shook her head.

'It's all right,' I reassured her. I rubbed with my thigh. She shook her head and was trying to say no.

'All right, I just thought...'

The door opened. A brunette entered, wearing a grey suit and a white blouse, looking very much the businesswoman. She stood looking at us and unbuttoning her jacket.

'Well now, isn't this interesting,' she said.

Her hair was pinned up, but she began to lower it, shaking her head so black hair fell to her shoulders. She was beautiful with a spectacular figure, her breasts and hips generously proportioned, her waist narrow. She stripped off the jacket and blouse. She was wearing a white satin slip, its lacy cups filled with creamy breasts. She unzipped her skirt and stepped out of it. The slip was split on one side almost to the waist, her long legs sheathed in champagne stockings with lacy welts.

'Well, look at you,' she said to the blonde. 'Don't you look good? I love the little dress. Very slutty, just how I wanted you.'

She rubbed the silk slip against her slave's body. 'Sarah, that's your name now, is that right?'

The blonde nodded.

'Are you having a good time?'

Sarah did not reply.

'Madam M tells me you can come home tomorrow. I've got everything prepared for you. But of course you don't know what I'm talking about, do you?'

Sarah shook her head.

'No, I forgot. Well, I'm Mistress Pamela. I'm your mistress. From now on you do exactly what I say. It looks as though Madam M's done wonders with you. She's trained you to obey me, isn't that so?'

Sarah nodded.

'Do you like feeling her body against you?'

Sarah shook her head.

'You ungrateful little wretch. Well, I think that deserves punishment, don't you?'

Sarah shook her head again and tried to say no. Mistress Pamela went to a cupboard and opened it. Inside I could see whips, riding crops and canes. She selected a riding crop as Sarah was twisting her head around to see what was happening.

'You know I'm going to enjoy disciplining you when we get home, Sarah. A little slut like you will need a lot of discipline.'

She practised slashing the crop through the air a few times, then positioned herself to the side of us. She measured her stroke, then thwacked the crop with brutal force against Sarah's vulnerable buttocks. Sarah screamed and jerked, lurching against me. Tears were in her eyes. She rested her head on my shoulder.

'Oh yes, that hurt,' Pamela said, before delivering three more strokes in quick succession, each making Sarah scream into the gag.

'That's enough of that,' Pamela said, almost to herself as she unclipped my wrists from the metal rings.

'Lie on the bed,' she said. 'On your stomach.'

I hurried to obey, not wanting the same treatment. I felt the woman kneel beside me, pull my wrists back and clip them together, then she told me to roll over onto my back, so my arms were trapped.

She straddled my head, facing Sarah, and I was enveloped in the white satin of her slip. I could see her sex. She wasn't wearing panties, her pubes dark and silky.

'I want you to watch me very carefully, Sarah,' I heard her say. 'If you take your eyes off me for one second it'll mean more punishment.'

I felt the satin lifting. She pulled the slip off over her head.

'You know what to do,' she said, lowering her wet sex onto my face.

Once again I was powerless to do anything but obey. I pushed my tongue up to her vagina, finding her clit already engorged. I heard her moan as I wriggled by tongue against the little nut, then moved it from side to side.

'Oh yes, like that,' Pamela cooed.

I felt her hands on my thighs, pulling them apart, and she leant forward and pressed her mouth to my exposed sex. I felt her fingers working under my thighs and into my vagina, pushing three fingers deep into my sex, making me gasp against her succulent, fragrant pussy, instantly unleashing a furious orgasm within me.

Her body reacted with violent spasms too. I felt her muscles tighten. She lifted her lips from my sex and let out a long cry of pleasure, before collapsing back on me, completely relaxed, like a rag doll.

After some minutes she stirred and rolled off me. She got to her feet, opened the chest of drawers at the side of the bed and took out a large dildo attached to a leather harness. It was very realistic, etched with veins just like the real thing.

58

Kneeling on the bed beside me she pulled the harness up over my legs and adjusted it so the dildo stuck up from my groin.

'Now you're going to watch while she fucks me,' Pamela said.

I looked at Sarah. She had a haggard look in her eyes and was staring down at me. I knew exactly the frustration she was feeling.

Mistress Pamela helped me to kneel up, then got onto all fours, facing Sarah, taunting her.

I shuffled closer, guessing what was expected of me. The dildo swayed and nudged against her buttocks.

She backed one hand between her legs and grabbed it, aiming the tip at her glistening vagina.

'Fuck me,' she ordered.

I moved my hips and watched the moulded shaft disappear into her sex, the lips taut around it. The flared base pressed against me and rubbed my clit, making me sigh with delight. Mistress Pamela was rapidly approaching another orgasm. And so was I. The resistance in her vagina became greater as it clenched around the phallus, and this in turn ground it harder against my clit. We both screamed as we shook with explosive orgasms.

'Well... they've certainly got you well trained,' she sighed, a few minutes later when we'd calmed down a bit. She removed the dildo and climbed off the bed. She took hold of my arm and pulled me up too, making me kneel behind Sarah. I watched as she peeled the hem of the mini-dress up over Sarah's hips, and was speechless by what she revealed. There was a lump inside her panties, up tight between her thighs, and it was obvious, even to me, what it was. Sarah was a man! Sarah's cock had been forced back between his legs and held tight there by something. No wonder she hadn't wanted me to push my thigh between her legs. I could just make out his scrotum, squeezed between his perineum and his cock.

'Suck it,' Pamela ordered.

Sarah immediately protested, trying to pull away from the bonds and shaking his head.

'Stop that or I'll have you spend another month here,' Pamela said.

I leant forward. Through the panties I pressed my lips to the glans, kissing it, sucking as best I could. I heard Sarah moan.

'This is how I found him,' Pamela said. 'In our bedroom with another transvestite tart trying on my lingerie. So I thought, if he wants to be a girl he can be my maid.'

Clearly Madam M's talents extended to feminising men, and there was no question that she had done an amazing job. Sarah was utterly convincing. I'd never doubted she was a girl.

'He's lucky I didn't have that cut off,' Pamela mused.

I concentrated on what I had been ordered to do. I sucked and felt Sarah's cock react, growing despite the bondage it was in. I wondered if he was going to come, going to ejaculate into the soft panties he wore.

Pamela watched as I sucked and licked as best I could, my face squeezed up between Sarah's parted thighs, my forehead against his bum.

'That's enough,' she eventually said.

I stopped, my cheeks flushed from my efforts, just as the bedroom door opened and Madam Celine entered.

'Have you finished with her?' she said tersely.

Mistress Pamela waved a dismissive hand in reply, and I was pulled to my feet and marched back downstairs.

Chapter Ten

Barbara didn't know what to do. As she settled into the back of the taxi she felt the throb of the two lashes that marked her bottom. Jack had dispensed corporal punishment before, but this was different. Usually he left no or little lasting evidence. But before leaving him and Tom she had seen in the mirror the welts on her bum were very visible and turning purple. She still shared a bedroom and a bathroom with Tony, so she would have to be very careful that he did not glimpse her backside.

It was late by the time she got home. Tony was not in the sitting room, so he was probably already in bed. Anxiously she climbed the stairs. He was in bed reading.

'How's June?' he asked.

'June...' She had almost forgotten the excuse she'd used. 'Oh June, right, they've made up.'

'Made up?'

'I told you. She and her husband were having a trial separation. Now he's back.'

'Is that a good idea?' he asked.

'That's what I said. She seems to think so.'

She had expected him to be sullen and annoyed that she'd cancelled dinner with him that night.

She went into the en-suite and began taking off her clothes, making sure her robe was right next to her should Tony decide to come in for a pee. Her panties were wet and she hid them at the bottom of the laundry basket.

She climbed into the shower, her back to the wall as a precaution. She soaped herself, then rinsed the lather away, savouring the warmth of the water for a while before stepping out of the cubicle. She wiped the steam off the large mirror and ruefully eyed the purple cross that marked her buttocks. Quickly she covered herself with a bath towel.

'Come to bed, darling,' Tony called. 'I've got a surprise for you.'

'Just a second.' She dried herself, slipped into her newly acquired black silk nightdress, then walked into the bedroom.

Tony had put down his book and thrown the covers aside. He had taken off his pyjamas and was lying with his erect cock in his hand.

'How about we play around?'

They hadn't had sex for at least a month, and only then for just a few minutes in the perfunctory missionary position. Why did he have to choose this night to want it again?

'I'm really tired, sweetie,' she said unconvincingly.

'I know. It's a long day for you. But I've been thinking about what great sex we always had. We've both been so busy we've let it slip. We need to be a bit more adventurous. A bit more creative.'

Barbara was trying to think quickly. If he took off her nightdress, and if his idea of being creative was to rekindle the days when his favourite way of fucking her was from behind, there was no way he wouldn't see the marks on her bum.

'Sounds lovely,' she said. 'I've got an idea.' She turned and went back into the bathroom, and took a bottle of massage oil from the cabinet.

Back in the bedroom she knelt on the bed and took his cock in her hand. 'Why don't you let me do that for you?' she purred as seductively as she could.

'Do you like that?'

'Mmm...'

She poured the oil over the head of his cock and massaged it in. He moaned again. She felt his cock throb.

'Why don't you let me do the same to you?' He moved his hand up her thigh.

'In a minute,' she said, hoping if she could make him ejaculate quickly he'd just want to go to sleep. 'Open your legs a bit more.'

She cupped his balls in one hand and squeezed gently, then leant forward and sucked them into her mouth, one by one. This was what he had always liked best. She began to wank him faster.

'That's great...' he moaned.

She pushed her other hand between his buttocks. The oil from his cock had run down over his anus, and when she pushed her middle finger into it there was little resistance. She wriggled her finger, searching for his prostate. Pushing against it she felt his cock throb violently. She fucked his anus with her finger, sucked his balls and wanked his cock. She needed to make him come, otherwise he'd want to fuck her, and almost certainly discover her little secret.

She felt his cock spasm, and thankfully an arc of spunk jetted from it and splashed her cheek. She milked every last drop from him, thick spunk oozing down over her fingers.

'That was great,' he panted. 'Let me do you now.'

'Don't be silly,' she said. 'That was so exciting I came too.'

'Did you?' For a second he looked quizzical, but then the late hour got the upper hand. 'OK, well goodnight then,' he said as he turned over onto his side, and within minutes was fast asleep.

The daily exercises got easier to perform, and it was difficult to keep my mind off sex. I thought a lot about Jack and the things he had done to me. In a way, what was happening now was just an extension of that. The mental anguish caused by the fact I was a prisoner held against my will did not seem to affect my physical being, and my body was in a constant state of arousal. There was enormous frustration too, and I would have given anything to have a man, or a woman, fuck me thoroughly. In bed at night I lay imagining what it would be like to be allowed to come, to have a hard cock spunking deep inside me, or to have a woman's mouth teasing my clit while she fucked me with a dildo. I couldn't get sex out of my mind.

If I'd been able to masturbate that would have brought some relief, but that was impossible, tied to the bed as I was. And to compound my frustration Madam Celine had also taken to locking me in a sort of chastity belt.

It was a simple enough device. A leather belt was buckled around my waist, from the front of which a hoop of steel passed down between my legs and up between my buttocks and fastened again to the belt in the small of my back. The steel was shaped so it was at its widest over my sex, then narrower between my bum cheeks.

Each morning when I woke I was finding it more and more difficult to remember who and where I was. I tried to keep myself awake for as long as I could, to avoid what I was sure was some sort of sleep treatment. As I lay there long into each night I couldn't hear anything that would indicate what the treatment was. I thought I heard a faint whispering voice, but it was too indistinct to work out what was being said. What I did know though was that the longer I slept the more difficult it was in the morning to recall the details of my life.

Then one night, whilst struggling as I always did to keep awake for as long as possible, I heard a key in the door and it opened.

'Are you awake?' a voice whispered.

'Yes,'

'Good.' The door closed again, returning the room to darkness. I felt a weight on the bed next to me.

'Who are you?' It definitely was not Madam Celine or Angel.

'Judy Bright.'

It meant nothing to me.

'Don't worry. I know. I've been watching you. You know who you are too, don't you?'

I hesitated; this might be a trap.

'It's all right, really. I'm just like you. I think they're giving us some sort of therapy. I don't know what. But mine didn't take properly. Yours didn't either, did it?'

'We shouldn't be talking like this,' I said defensively. 'How did you get out of your cell?'

'I used to work on cruise ships with a magician. He did a lot of escapology. I managed to find a safety pin. The locks they use on the cuffs are easy and the door is too, once you know how. Do you want me to undo you?'

'Is this a trap?'

Judy laughed quietly. 'I know why you would think that. I just thought we could plan a way to get out of here. Look, I was unfaithful to my husband, he found me with my lover. He was furious, especially because it was a woman. Here, let me undo those.'

The padlocks on the cuffs clicked open. I lowered my arms, but was still suspicious.

'Have you heard it?'

'Heard what?'

'The voice in the night. It's what's making everyone so compliant. Some sort of sleep therapy.'

'I thought I heard something, but it was very faint.'

'Right. Mine too. But because I could get myself up off the bed I managed to find the speaker. Put my ear right next to it. It's some sort of hypnosis, I guess. But I think my speaker's not working properly. Looks like yours has got the same problem. That's why we're OK.'

That made sense. I was beginning to trust Judy.

'So, tell me what happened to you,' she urged.

I told her. It was a relief to tell someone what had happened. It all came pouring out. Perhaps I should have held back some of the details, but I didn't. I told her everything. I told her what Jack had done to me, and how I'd come to love it and yearn for it. She didn't seem at all surprised.

'Yes,' she said, 'I think you and I are very similar.'

'How so?' I asked.

'Because I had the same experience, except with a woman not a man. Like yours my marriage had got very lazy in the bed department. We just didn't do it much. He didn't seem interested and even when he was it was over in a couple of minutes. I can't say I really minded that much. Sex just didn't seem that important.'

'Right,' I said. 'That was the same with me.'

'Then I met Helen. I used to go to these exercise classes twice a week and one day, well it just happened.'

'What did?'

'I was coming out of an aerobics class and I saw this woman. She was black, and tall. I don't think I'd ever seen anything like her. She was dressed in a leather catsuit and thigh boots and she had incredibly long legs. The catsuit was so tight it cut up between her legs and folded into her sex. I mean, you could see everything. Her hair was cropped short and she had big boobs. The catsuit had a zip all the way down the front, and she'd pulled it down so a lot of her cleavage was on display.

'I'd never in my life looked at a woman sexually, but there I was, just standing and staring with my mouth open. I followed her before I knew what I was doing. She walked around the corner and into an apartment building. At the front door, as she got her keys out, she turned and asked me if I was following her. I blushed and said I was. She didn't bat an eyelid, like it was something that happened to her all the time. She invited me in. She had this really fantastic penthouse on the top floor.

'Well I didn't really know what I was doing. It all felt a bit like a dream. She gave me a glass of wine, told me her name was Helen, then asked me what I wanted. I just didn't know what to say. There was only one word I could think of. Sex. I wanted sex. I babbled something about finding her very attractive. She looked at me critically for a moment. She had these amazing dark brown eyes. What you want, she said, is to have sex with me. I just nodded. I can't tell you how I felt. My heart was beating ten to the dozen.

'Well, she said, you've chosen the wrong person, unless you're submissive. I told her I didn't know what she meant. She got to her feet and said I'd better leave it there, and started to show me to the door.

'Look, she said, if you want the truth I'm a life style dominatrix. That means I only have sex with submissives; women and men who are prepared to obey me without question.

'It was weird because I felt myself getting all hot and bothered. For some reason what she was saying made me even more excited. I stuttered that I didn't mind what she did to me, but she looked sceptical.

'All right, she said, and told me I'd only have one chance. If I disobeyed her, if I did the slightest thing she didn't like, I'd have to leave and she would never see me again.

'I agreed. Half of me thought I must be mad, but the half that was almost dizzy with excitement was in charge.

'Well then, she said, we'd better get on with it. She took one step towards me, put her hand around the back of my neck and kissed me full on the lips, her tongue plunging deep into my mouth while her thigh forced its way between my legs. I had never kissed a woman before and it astonished me that I felt such intense passion. I kissed her back, pressing my lips against hers and entwining my tongue into her mouth. The feel of her breasts against mine was another huge thrill.

'She told me to follow her. We walked down the hall and she opened a door at the end. She asked if I was sure I wanted to go in. Believe me I was sure. My sex was wet and my nipples so hard.

'It was a fairly ordinary bedroom, although the bed was covered in a black rubber sheet. There was a cupboard against one wall, but the oddest thing was what was hanging from two chains in the ceiling. It was a piece of wood, about a foot tall by four feet wide. Three holes were cut in it, two smaller ones and a larger one in the middle, like stocks, from the olden days.

'Helen told me to take my clothes off, all of them. For a moment I hesitated, but she reminded me that if I didn't I'd never see her again.

'I was wearing a skirt and blouse, bra, panties and tights. I took them all off while Helen watched my every move. She then pulled me over to the suspended stocks. The wood was hinged and she opened it up and bent me into it, so my neck was in the central hole and my wrists in the smaller ones. She closed the wood around me and fastened it with a clasp and a padlock. I feared what I'd let myself in for, but my excitement pushed everything else aside.

'She strapped two cuffs around my ankles. She pulled my legs apart and clipped the cuffs to rings in the floor, so my legs were spread wide. I was powerless. I knew my sex was exposed and she would see I was excited. I waited. My field of vision was severely restricted.

'I heard Helen move, there was a whistling sound and my backside exploded with pain. I gasped, speechless. She hit me again, a new line burning across my poor bum. Then another and another. I was in a terrible state because the pain turned to this feverish kind of pleasure, and I realised I was going to come. I didn't understand how or why. I had never experienced anything like it, and as the whip or whatever it was lashed down again an orgasm like nothing I'd ever felt before just crashed through me.

'Helen knew what had happened and stopped. She said nothing and I heard her walk out of the room, leaving me there, in the stocks, shattered by the enormity of my climax and what she'd done to me. I found it hard to come to terms with it all. I was tied to a peculiar bondage contraption in a strange room where I'd been whipped to an orgasm by a black dominatrix.

'I don't know how long she left me there, but when she came back she was naked apart from a pair of black high-heels. She had a sort of spandex hood in her hand, which she pulled over my head. It was tight, with no holes for my eyes or mouth, though I could breathe through the material. I felt her hand on my bum. Both hands caressed me and I could feel the welts from the beating tingling in a way that took my breath away. Her fingers opened my pussy and she touched my clit. I was really wet. Without saying a word she rubbed my clit, and I was coming again in seconds. I couldn't help but scream with pleasure.

'I don't know whether she left the room again or just stood watching me. After only a few minutes I felt the ankle cuffs being unstrapped, the stocks being opened and my head and wrists freed. She pulled my arms behind my back and used rope to tie my wrists together. She also tied my elbows, forcing my breasts out. I was told to lie face down on the bed, then she used more rope to tie my ankles and knees together. I had never been tied up before. It was another new experience for me. Helen knelt on the bed and pulled off the hood. Then she rolled me onto my back and straddled my face.

'Lying on my back my burning buttocks were exposed to the cool of the rubber sheet, and it felt really good. I stared up at Helen's sex. She lowered herself onto my mouth. I licked, and found her clit. I was gratified to hear her gasp, and felt her quiver with excitement as she pressed down on my mouth. In return I felt a finger tease my clit. She knew just what to do. She stroked with a perfect rhythm and pressure. I tried to do the same for her but I lost myself to another exquisite orgasm.

'Well, I don't know what time I got home that night. Fortunately my husband took little notice of me and I always wore pyjamas in bed, otherwise he might have thought it strange that my bum was striped in colours ranging from red to purple.'

'You saw her again?' I asked.

'I couldn't wait. She told me never to call her. She took my email and told me she'd be in touch when it was convenient for her. I had to wait a week, and by the end of it I was a nervous wreck. I was like an addict wanting a drug.'

'Exactly. That's what I felt,' I said, remembering only too clearly what had happened with Jack. 'So what happened then?'

'The second time?'

'Yes.'

'Well I got this email telling me to arrive at exactly six o'clock that night. She only gave me four hours' notice. I was nervous as a kitten. I got myself tarted up this time, in a satin corset and black seamed stockings and my highest heels. I thought about whether I should wear panties but decided I wouldn't. I wore a tight red dress which hardly reached my stockings and showed plenty of boob, and spent an hour doing my make-up.

'Helen opened the door wearing a body-stocking in sheer black nylon, with thong panties and high-heeled shoes. Her boobs were squeezed by the tightness of the material, and her nipples were already erect.

'She took me straight into the room at the end of the hall. She guided me over to the bed and told me to take my dress off. She smiled when she saw the corset and stockings.

'There was a broad leather belt on the rubber sheet. She ordered me to kneel on it, then pulled each end around the tops of my thighs and buckled it tightly so my heels were squeezed into my bottom and my legs were doubled up under me. Then she pushed my torso down so my breasts touched my thighs. She took another longer belt, worked it under my shins and up around my back, buckling it there and pinning my arms to my sides. She'd made me into a neat little ball.

'She knelt by my bowed head. She pulled a rubber helmet down over it. There were no holes for my mouth or my eyes, but there were two holes for my nostrils. I felt her fingers in front of my lips. There was some sort of flap on the inside of the helmet and she fed it into my mouth. Suddenly the rubber began to inflate between my lips, pushing my tongue down and my cheeks out. I was alarmed at first.

'I felt her weight lifting from the bed and then there was silence. I listened intently for some clue as to what she had in mind for me, but there was no sound. I had the feeling she was looking at me, but it was possible she'd left the room, like she did the last time.

'My alarm was rapidly replaced by excitement. My body seemed to respond to bondage. I could see myself on the bed, rolled into a tight ball by the belts, my buttocks exposed, my naked sex pressed between them, my head encased in black rubber. I knew I was wet and leaking onto my bare thighs.

'The whistle caught me unawares and I had no time to tense my bum against the pain. I jerked but the belts contained the movement and all I managed to do was rock on the bed. The gag muffled my scream.

'Another stroke fell and I experienced another convulsion, but now I hardly registered pain, only extreme pleasure. The position I was in, the inescapable bondage, and the fact that I could not see or speak, only concentrated my senses on what I was feeling. I knew I was coming, as quickly and as intensely as the first time she whipped me. I came on the fourth stroke, but even though I was shuddering and squealing with delight she didn't stop. More strokes fell and the last one seemed to take my orgasm to another level.

'Tied as I was it was difficult to draw breath, and it took a long time for me to recover. But when finally my breathing calmed and my senses returned I was aware of Helen kneeling next to me on the bed. A hand stroked my bum and provoked new shards of sensation, but before I could react it withdrew.

'I felt her move, then her hands were gripping my hips and something large and hard was nudging into me. I knew what it was, but it was only when it entered so deep I could feel her against my buttocks that I realised she'd strapped a dildo on and was fucking me with it.

'Her thrusts became more and more urgent. I could feel her excitement. I could hear her breathing in time with her movements, her fingers digging into the leather that held me so tightly. Then she stopped and pulled me right back onto her cock, and I heard a long, slow sigh.

'It seemed a long time before she moved again. She pulled off the rubber helmet. I blinked and saw her kneeling in front of me. She had a harness buckled around her hips and a big black dildo extended from it, glistening wet. She pulled my head up and pushed the dildo into my mouth. I tasted my own juices as she ordered me to suck it.

'She took off the harness. She pulled the dildo from my mouth and lay back on the bed, her legs spread out on either side of my balled body. The body stocking had a slit which exposed her thong. She worked herself forward, spreading her legs apart then draping them over my back so her pussy was pressed against my mouth.

'Well that was it, really. I was hooked. I could hardly think of anything else. Sex with my husband had become such a rare event that he didn't notice the welts frequently decorating my backside.

'Then about two months later he went away on a business trip for a weekend. It was quite sudden and unexpected. By this time Helen had allowed me to email her, so I took the opportunity to ask her round to the house, and she agreed.

'As usual I was feeling incredibly randy and as usual I got dressed for the occasion, in a red waspie, red stockings and matching ankle boots with high heels. I wore a red robe which did little to hide my tits and my pussy.

'She arrived at the appointed hour. She wore a black leather suit with tight trousers and calf length boots, matching the leather holdall she carried.

'Helen never showed an interest in small-talk. She was only interested in sex. So without a word she put the holdall on one of the hall chairs and unzipped it, taking out a coil of black rope. I was ordered to stand facing the stair balustrade with my hands up above my head, while she went up a few steps. With the rope she tied my raised wrists to the polished wood handrail.

'She took off her jacket. She wasn't wearing a blouse or a bra and her lovely boobs were naked. With sensuous movements she peeled the trousers off, wearing nothing underneath.

'She came back down, behind me, pressing her body against mind while her hands circled my breasts. Her fingers took hold of my nipples and pinched them, making me yelp.

'She stepped back and raised the whip. I felt my buttocks tingle in anticipation, and then she thwacked the whip across them. Five strokes followed, hard strokes that made me gasp and shudder with pleasure. By the last I was again trembling as I climaxed.

She discarded the whip and took a harness and dildo from the holdall, slipped it over her hips and moved towards me. I felt the dildo touch my buttocks then dip down between my legs. In moments it was deep inside me. She appeared impatient and began thrusting into me, panting softly with each inward stroke.

'And that was when the front door opened. I think I screamed. My husband was smiling, the smug bastard, and I realised he'd known exactly what had been going on. He'd told me he was going away as a trap and I'd fallen right into it.

'He pulled Helen back, picked up the whip and stroke it down my buttocks. I shall never forget that feeling. Minutes before the same thing had produced unbelievable ecstasy, but now all I felt was shame. I begged him to stop and let me down, but instead he whipped me.'

'So what happened after that?'

'Helen got dressed and left. I think she felt a bit guilty at getting me into trouble, but it wasn't her fault. I wanted it. My husband told me I was a lesbian bitch and he wanted a divorce.'

'And?'

'He changed his mind. After a couple of weeks he told me it was partly his fault for neglecting me.'

'That's what Tony told me.'

'Right. He said we should go and see a marriage counsellor.'

'Madam M.'

'Exactly. I think she tried to hypnotise me. It didn't really work. Well I fell asleep, but when I woke up I knew who I was even though they kept telling me I didn't.'

'That's it. That's what happened to me.' Any doubts I might have had about Judy had disappeared. I felt a great feeling of relief. Now I had an ally. Perhaps we would be able to get out of the place together. 'So what do we do now?'

'We have to get out of here.'

'But how? I've been looking for a way but we're always in bondage and locked in these rooms.'

'That's not the biggest problem,' Judy said. 'I can deal with the locks, that's the easy bit. It's the door at the top of the stairs that's the problem. It's bolted, top and bottom. Unless someone unbolts it from the other side we can't get out of the cellar.'

'There must be a way. We pretend they've succeeded with us and then they'll let us go back to our so-called masters.'

'I don't think that's going to work,' she said. 'There's a sort of evaluation test at the end of the treatment. I don't think we could beat it unless we're really under, and if we don't they're not going to let us go.'

'Well then, we just have to hope someone's forgetful with the bolts one night.'

Chapter Eleven

Another stolen evening. That's how she thought of it. Tony was working late at the office. She told him she was going to the cinema with a friend. That way he wouldn't be suspicious if her phone was turned off. In the taxi she was feeling her usual mounting excitement.

She'd spent a great deal of time shopping online for lingerie she hoped would please him. She'd found a black rubber corset with shoulder straps and suspenders that clung to her like a second skin. And most daringly, it had two holes for her breasts that left them completely exposed. She wore rubber stockings and thong rubber panties too. The company she'd bought it from sent a bottle of liquid which, applied to the rubber, made it shiny and bright. She'd spent most of the afternoon polishing the kinky outfit.

Arriving, she went through the usual routine of ringing the downstairs bell. She let herself into the flat and went into the cloakroom. She took her dress off and looked at herself in the mirror. The holes in the corset were tight and the constriction around her breasts had made them pink and her nipples stiffen. As she got on all fours to crawl down the hall - a humiliation that still left her breathless with excitement - she could feel the lips of her sex wet inside the non-absorbent rubber panties.

The door of the black room was open. He was standing inside naked, erection in hand.

'Rubber, is it? Very kinky. You'd better come in.'

As usual she was unable to think of anything to say.

'I've been planning something special for you tonight. Stand up.'

She did as she was told, staring at his cock.

'Turn around,' he said. 'Cross your wrists behind your back.'

She obeyed. He moved behind her. She felt something hard and cold slipping around her wrists, locking together.

He sat on the bed and pulled her down on his lap, positioning her over his knee like a naughty child. She could feel his erection pressing against her side.

His hand caressed her upturned buttocks. She felt his fingers slip between her legs and under the rubber panties, sampling how excited she was by his domineering treatment.

Suddenly he raised his hand and spanked her. She yelped. He spanked her again, the flat of his hand swatting her toned globes. She felt his cock throb against her side as each blow fell. Over and over again his hand battered her buttocks. It was a feeling like no other. Her bum was on fire. She felt herself tense, sweating inside the humid confines of the corset, her sex seeping juices, yet again such treatment bringing her to the point of a mind-blowing orgasm.

She lost count of how many times he spanked her, but when he stopped he was breathing heavily. Fingers unhooked the suspenders, then moved inward and down to her pussy. If she was not so turned on she would have blushed with embarrassment at how wet she was. His fingers entered her and pushed deep, his knuckles pressing against her clit, and that tipped her into another extraordinary orgasm that had her shuddering and sobbing, draped over his lap.

Jack slid her off his knee onto the floor. He opened his legs and pulled her up so she was kneeling between them, his erection spearing up from his lap.

'My turn,' he said.

She sucked his cock into her mouth and was gratified to hear him moan as she sank down to the root. She could feel his cock straining, and knew he was already close to ejaculating. Spanking and frigging her had clearly turned him on as much as it had her.

She moved her mouth up and down his shaft, sucking and licking. She heard him moan, which thrilled her. She used her tongue to wriggle against the underside of his glans. He moaned again. She plunged down on him until he was right at the back of her throat, then felt his cock begin to spasm and thick jets of spunk erupting as he gasped with pleasure. Eagerly she swallowed every drop. It was the first time he'd allowed himself to come in her mouth.

She didn't expect him to praise her, and he didn't. He took hold of her arm and helped her to her feet.

'Now you're going to get me hard again,' he said. He pushed her down onto the bed so she was lying on her back. He took a large dildo from the small chest of drawers at the side of the bed.

'Open your legs. You're going to entertain me.'

She did as she was told. He knelt beside her and fed the dildo into her vagina in one smooth movement. He left it embedded in her and began to play with his cock, wanking slowly.

She loved displaying herself to him like this and could feel his eyes taking in every detail of her. With her arms pinned beneath her there was little she could do but lie there, watching him watching her.

He twisted the switch and she moaned as the motor buzzed and the vibrations spread through her sex. She felt her clit pulse deliciously. At that moment she existed only for him. That was all she cared about. She would do anything he asked. She gasped as another orgasm rippled through her, her breasts quivering as she spasmed and trembled, her mouth open, her eyes shut.

'Would you like me to fuck you?' she heard him say.

'Oh yes, please...'

'Hold your new friend where it is,' he said, 'and turn over on to your stomach.'

She obeyed with difficulty, managing to roll over and keep the dildo in place as he told her to.

She felt him moving, then fingers parted her buttocks and coated her anus with lubricant. She knew at once what he intended.

He seized her by the hips and pulled her up onto her knees, her forehead resting on the bed, her hands bound in the small of her back. She felt his erection prod against her rear opening. For a moment she went rigid and her anus contracted, but the thought of that delicious cock sinking into her forbidden passage overcame her apprehension and she relaxed. His glans stretched her. Barbara winced with the discomfort, but it quickly turned into intense pleasure. She found herself pressing back against him, wanting more, wanting his cock deep, deep inside her.

Jack gave her what she wanted. His fingers dug into her hips and his penis plunged into her rectum. Again there was pain, but there was also the most extraordinary bliss. It was such an overwhelming sensation that she knew she was going to come. She felt her vagina convulse and her anus contract, squeezing Jack's cock and creating a whole new swathe of delight. She sobbed as her body catapulted her into another orgasm, inner muscles locked around the two rigid phalluses entrenched in her depths.

She felt Jack begin to move. He thrust with his groin and holding the dildo he thrust with that too. She felt his cock swell, stretching the walls of her rear passage even more, and as she flowed into yet another orgasm he came too, his spunk bathing the dark recesses of her most private place.

'So this is your little love nest, is it? And you must be lover boy.'

Tony's voice cut through her like a knife.

Chapter Twelve

Something woke me. I shook my head and opened my eyes. The door to my cell had been opened and there was a thin beam of light searching the room.

'Barbara?' The light came from a small torch. It shone on my face, dazzling me. 'Barbara, is that you?'

A weight settled on the bed next to me.

'Jeez, what have they done to you?'

The torchlight played on my bonds, the way my hands were cuffed to the bed above my head, and the chastity belt. 'He's had your nipples pierced! Barbara, it's me, Jack.' He shone the torchlight on his own face.

Jack. My heart was racing. 'Jack?' I said. 'How did you get in here?'

'I phoned the house. I got your housekeeper. She was worried about you. She told me she hadn't seen you for weeks. Your husband told her you'd gone to stay with your sister. I rang your sister and she didn't know anything about it. I knew Tony was up to something. He had you sent here.'

'Weeks?' I'd lost count of the days I had been here. 'But how did you find me?'

'I'll tell you later when we have more time. Right now, we've got to get out of here.'

'They're working some sort of conditioning, with hypnosis or something. Thankfully it didn't work on me. I've been trying to find a way to get out but there isn't one. How did you know which cell I was in?'

'Apparently I was the first door he opened.' I looked beyond Jack and could just make out the naked shape of Judy in the doorway. 'I showed him the way.'

She came in and unlocked the cuffs and the chastity belt, which we took off after I got up off the bed on rather stiff limbs.

'Have they given you any drugs?' Jack asked.

'No, I don't think so,' Judy replied. 'It's some sort of hypnotherapy they do at night. There's others here, men and women. The aim is to turn us all into obedient sex slaves.'

'Jesus. I'm so sorry Barbara. I got you into all this, didn't I? It's all my fault.'

'Well now you can get me out of it,' I said.

'If I hadn't approached you at that party... you were happy with Tony.'

'No Jack, I wasn't,' I reassured him. 'If wasn't you it would have ended up being someone else. I was just kidding myself I was happy. Tony's an absolute bastard. I mean, look what he's been willing to do to me.'

'OK, well let's get you out of here. First we've got to find you some clothes. Any ideas?'

'Judy knows her way around best.'

'They make us wear catsuits,' Judy said. 'I know where they are.'

Jack trained the torchlight up and down the corridor, then Judy led the way to a cupboard set into the wall. She opened it and took out two of the rubber catsuits.

'Here,' she said, handing me one.

I started to struggle with it. Luckily there was enough talcum powder residue to make pulling them on a little easier, but it took at least ten minutes before we'd got the whole suit in place while we listened anxiously for any sound.

'I got in over the garden wall at the back,' Jack said. 'Follow me.'

We walked upstairs and he led the way through the familiar corridors until we got to a room I'd never been in. It was a large sitting room with French windows looking onto the garden. I could see marks on the door where Jack had forced it open. He led us out onto the lawn, his torch a narrow beam of light on the grass. We ran across to a large tree, its branches extending out over the garden wall. It was comparatively easy to climb it and shin along a branch, then drop down on the other side.

Jack's car was parked in the lane ten yards away. We were free.

'Where are we?' I asked.

'Tring. Come on, we have to get out of here. You'd better scrunch down. You're likely to get arrested if anyone sees you in those outfits.'

Luckily when we got to Jack's apartment building there didn't appear to be any neighbours about, so we rushed across the foyer to the lift. It was only once we were in his flat and he was guiding us into the bedroom that I really felt safe. Safe, and incredibly horny. The idea of being with Jack again, despite all the trouble he'd got me into, made my hormones go wild.

I caught him in my arms and kissed him.

'Thank you,' I said.

'Don't thank me, it was my fault.' He seemed genuinely upset, concern etched into his face.

'Jack, I don't care. We'll talk about it in the morning. Now there's one thing you've got to do for me and fast. I don't care how you do it or what you want to do with me but you've got to fuck me, and fuck me now.'

He looked at Judy. The catsuit clung to every contour of her delicious body.

'I'll go, if I can find some clothes,' she said.

'No,' I said firmly. 'Stay tonight at least. She can stay, can't she Jack?'

'Of course.'

'Have you got a guestroom?' she asked.

'No,' I said again. I stepped out of Jack's arms and into hers. I kissed her firmly, our naked breasts squashing together. 'I want you to thank him properly too,' I said.

I took her hand and led her to the bed. My sudden freedom appeared to have liberated my libido too. I lay on the bed and pulled her on top of me, kissing her ferociously again and running my hands all over her. I knew how much Jack liked to watch two women together. The rubber was smooth and slippery and I soon wriggled down over her body and pulled her legs apart so I could get my mouth on her sex, exposed by the slit in the rubber.

'I thought you'd want to rest,' Jack said.

'I want to fuck.'

I began to tongue Judy's clitoris. The nights we'd spent together had taught me what she liked. I felt her body tense and she moaned.

I realised that this was the first time in Jack's presence that I'd taken the initiative and not waited to be ordered to do what he wanted. I heard him stripping off his clothes and felt him kneeling on the bed behind me. He gripped my hips and pulled them up until my sex was level with his cock. He thrust eagerly.

The feeling of his cock inside me almost gave me an orgasm. But tonight what mattered was what I wanted. And I didn't want to come yet. I pulled away from him and wriggled around on the bed until I could take him in my mouth. His cock was slick with my juices and I licked hungrily.

I pulled away for a moment. 'Fuck her, Jack,' I said. 'I want you to give her a really good time.'

He didn't hesitate. He buried his cock in Judy's cunt, pounding her while she screamed encouragement with a string of obscenities.

I watched the muscles in his buttocks contracting as he drove deeper and I used my own fingers in my pussy.

'Oh yes, yes, fuck me,' Judy screamed, her hands clutching at Jack's back, her legs raised so her knees were almost back to her shoulders. I could see the whole of his cock disappearing inside her and his balls rolling against her puckered anus, her juices making her sex glisten.

'Fuck her,' I repeated insistently. It felt so strange to be giving orders.

'Oh yes, that feels sooo good,' Judy moaned.

I ran a hand over his buttocks and used two fingers to penetrate his arse.

'Jeez! What are you doing now?' he hissed, twisting his head to look around at me. I felt his anus clench as his cock spasmed, Judy's body shuddering beneath him as he filled her with spunk.

Now it was my turn. The sight of her orgasm had made me even more hungry for my own. With one hand concentrating on my clit I slid two fingers of the other deep into my vagina. In seconds I was coming, my eyes riveted on Judy's sex, still penetrated by Jack's cock and leaking some of his sperm.

A little while later Jack was lounging on the bed, his cock soft and of little use to me.

'Turn over,' I said, 'on your front.'

He looked puzzled. Previously I'd always been the ultimate submissive, meek and obedient, but that part of my personality had changed.

'Do as I say,' I snapped, enjoying my new role.

He did. I winked at Judy, who was also looking at me with amazement. I picked up one of his riding crops.

'I hope you can take it as well as dish it out,' I said, slashing the crop down on his buttocks. He yelped as the thwack of leather on flesh filled the small room. A red line appeared on the white flesh.

'What's got into you?' he asked, taken aback.

'This is what I want.'

I slashed the whip down again. I could see Judy's eyes sparkling with excitement.

'If this is your way of thanking him for rescuing you I think I should thank him too,' she said, smiling.

I gave her the whip. She raised it and slashed it down on his reddening buttocks twice in quick succession. Jack gasped.

'Now let's see whether he likes it,' I said. I pulled Jack over onto his back. His cock was fully erect. I seized it in my hand and without hesitation straddled his hips and sank down on it. It was my turn to gasp, my vagina moulding to the contours of Jack's cock.

'Feels good, doesn't it?' Judy said, clearly seeing in my eyes what I was experiencing. She took my breasts in her hands, kneading them and pinching my nipples. She straddled Jack's head and lowered herself onto his lips, his face smothered between her slender thighs.

I concentrated on my own pleasure. As Judy's fingers played with my nipples I began to move up and down, a few inches at first and then more deeply until I was pulling myself almost off him then plunging down again, the feeling of being penetrated, of that sword of hot flesh forcing its way into the deepest recesses of my body, taking me to new heights of passion. I was panting for breath and every nerve in my body was connected to the orgasm that exploded in me, making me scream with pure pleasure. Somewhere I could hear another female voice with the same intensity, but only dimly realised that Judy was coming too.

As I regained my composure I was astonished at the way I had behaved. It seemed that being unexpectedly freed from bondage my mind had decided to assert itself, and was determined to get what it wanted.

I smiled dreamily at Judy, who had climbed off Jack and was curled up on the bed beside him, obviously as exhausted as I was. Jack went off to shower. I had no memory of him coming back. All I remember is spooning up to Judy, putting my arm around her and falling asleep.

For breakfast Judy and I had croissants and coffee in Jack's kitchen, while he went out to buy us both some clothes. When he returned Judy slipped into a pair of jeans, a T-shirt and trainers and thanked him. He invited her to stay but she said she had things to do. I imagined that the man who had put her into training was going to have some very unpleasant surprises before the day was out.

'OK,' I said, 'so Tony had me sent to that place to have me turned into some kind of zombie sex slave. But how did he know of its existence?'

'Look, you know I've dabbled in S&M for a while. There's a lot of clubs out there and occasionally I've been to one or two. That's where I met Sandra. She's really into it.'

I felt a pulse of excitement and jealousy at the same time.

'Well when I told her about what had happened she made some inquiries. She found out about Melanie. Melanie Masters she calls herself, though I doubt that's her real name.'

'And?'

'Apparently some of the dominants at the club wanted to take things further with their submissives. She had a doctorate in psychology and she reckoned she'd found a way to wipe out memory. Sandra used to have a permanent master and he told her all about it. You have to have a lot of money.'

'I guessed that, but does it really work?'

'Apparently. And judging from her lifestyle Melanie makes a lot of money out of it.'

'So that's how you found me?'

'Yes. Sandra got me the number and I phoned her. I think they made a few checks on me then I was invited to the house. I was pretty certain that's where you were.'

'And while you were there you took advantage of the facilities?'

'I might have,' he grinned. 'I had to make my interest appear genuine.'

'So it looks like I've got a lot to thank Sandra for.'

'I'm sure we can find a way for you to do that. But first...'

'What?'

'There's something else.'

'What?'

'You own half the shares in his company, don't you?'

'No, more than half. It used to be owned by my father. He gave it to me in his will. Tony has options on some shares but the majority belong to me.'

'That makes it even worse.'

'What do you mean?'

'I've got a friend who works in the City. Tony's planning a management buy-out. His management.'

'He can't do that without my shares.'

'Exactly. He's called a shareholder's meeting. With you all obedient and submissive he'll order you to vote for the motion and the buy-out will go through on the nod. Completely legal and above board. Then the company would be his and your shares would be less than worthless.'

'The bastard. I'd end up with nothing.'

'Exactly.'

I thought for a moment. If I revealed to Tony that my memory had never been affected and his plans for me hadn't worked we'd no doubt have a huge row and I'd tell him to leave. But when it came to his plans for what was basically my company he could deny everything and pretend nothing had been going on. Of course I could vote him out of his job at the shareholder's meeting but the company would still have to pay him a compensation package, and after what he'd done I didn't want him to get a penny. If everyone found out what he was planning he'd be humiliated and have no alternative but to resign. So I needed to have him go through with the whole scheme until it suited me to reveal my hand.

'I think I know exactly what I'm going to do.'

'You've got to stop him.'

'Oh, I will.' I said. Thoughts were spinning in my head. I had to think fast.

I decided I couldn't wait. If Tony still believed I was his mindless slave I had a plan I thought might work, but I had to act fast. If I disappeared for any length of time then turned up with no warning he would be suspicious. I had to make him believe my escape had been an accident and that nothing else had changed.

I told Jack what I had in mind and he agreed it was the only way.

We waited until the afternoon, then Jack dropped me off close to my house, careful to make sure no one saw us. I hid the coat he had leant me under some bushes in the front garden and sat on the front doorstep wearing the rubber catsuit I had hurriedly put on for my escape. Thankfully the garden wall hid the porch from the road so no passers-by could see the strange sight of a woman in rubber waiting outside her own house.

I'd had time to think about what he had done to me and what he was planning to do. Of course it was my fault I'd had an affair. It was also my fault that I'd got caught. But having me kidnapped, locked up with the view to wiping my memory and training me as a sexual robot as well as planning to steal my money was taking revenge one step too far.

It was late in the afternoon and I knew Tony would get back from the office at any moment. I looked down at my naked breasts, the gold rings in my nipples prominent, the flesh already reddened by the constriction of the rubber. My nipples were erect.

It was little more than five minutes later when his car pulled into the driveway. Quickly I got to my knees, my hands behind my back and my head bowed.

I heard Tony giving the driver instructions for tomorrow then footsteps approached over the gravel.

'Good grief...!' Tony exclaimed. 'What on earth are you doing here?'

'I don't know, master,' I said, my head still bowed.

'What do you mean you don't know?'

'I don't know, master,' I repeated. 'I was frightened. Someone came in the night. I thought it was a test of obedience so I went with him. He took me and another woman to a strange house. There was another man there. He was very cross. Then they brought me here.'

'How did they know to bring you here?'

'I don't know, master. I don't know. I don't know where I am. When they took us to the strange house the man said they were supposed to take two women but I was the wrong one. Then he told them to bring me here.'

'You don't recognise this house?'

'No, master.'

'She has done a good, job,' Tony said, almost to himself.

He opened the front door, pulled me to my feet and shoved me inside. He pulled me through to the living room.

'Wait here.'

I fell to my knees again, pursuant to my supposed training.

He took out his mobile phone and punched in a number. 'Hello. Melanie. She's here. I don't know what happened. She says they said something about taking the wrong girl. But how would they know to bring her here?'

This was the only flaw in my story and my whole plan could fall apart if Madam M didn't come up with some explanation. I held my breath.

He listened for a moment. 'What, you don't even lock the files away? Well they must have got into your office and looked at them. That's the only way they could have found out where she lives. You'd better tighten up your security. And what about the other woman? What's going on?' He listened again. 'So she's still missing? Is that a problem?' What he heard seemed to reassure him. 'No, no, she looks just the same. She thought it was some sort of obedience test. I'll make sure I keep her under lock and key just in case. You said you were planning to hand her over to me on Friday, so if you agree I might as well keep her here.' He listened again then said, 'Fine, I'll call you tomorrow.'

He hung up and put the phone down. I breathed a sigh of relief.

Tony pulled me to my feet. He guided me upstairs to our bedroom. I noticed there was a blue teddy hanging from the wardrobe door - and it wasn't mine. It looked like Tony had taken full advantage of my absence. I tried to be careful not to betray myself by recognising where we were. He opened the wardrobe and took out two of his leather belts.

'Put your hands behind your back,' he said.

I did as I was told. He wrapped one of the leather belts around my wrists, binding them behind my back. He buckled it tight, the leather biting into my flesh. He stripped off his suit and the rest of his clothes.

'Now lean over with your head on the bed,' he said.

Again I obeyed. He'd whipped me in this position when I'd been with Angela. His hands caressed my buttocks.

'This is what you like, isn't it, Nat?'

'If it pleases you, master,' I said.

He raised the belt and swept it down against my poor bum. The familiar rush of pleasurable pain made me moan.

He struck four more times then threw the belt on the bed. He was now fully erect, the tip of his penis leaking pre-cum. The whipping had excited him just as much as the first time, but now there was no Angela for him to fuck and taunt me with.

He lay on the bed. 'I want you to come here and suck me,' he said.

'Yes, master. Thank you.'

I knelt on the bed. I crawled between his legs and lowered my mouth to his cock, swallowing it and sucking obediently.

'Oh yeah...' he sighed smugly.

I lifted until he was almost out of my mouth, then sank down again, massaging his cock with my lips and tongue. I heard him moan, but I heard something else too. Footsteps coming up the stairs. I heard the bedroom door opening.

'What's she doing here?' It was a woman's voice.

From the corner of my eye I saw him put a finger to his lips to indicate silence.

'Oh, I see,' the woman said. 'I thought you said Friday.'

'I did. Some guy broke in and took her but he got the wrong girl.'

'What guy?'

'How should I know? It was obviously some botched rescue attempt. Someone trying to get his girl back, is my guess.'

'Is she good at that?'

'She's been specially trained.'

I still couldn't see her but I felt her behind me.

'Have you just whipped her?' she asked.

'She loves it.'

The woman's fingers stroked down between my legs, then pushed into my sex.

'She's very wet.'

'That's what whipping does. Melanie trains them to associate pain and pleasure.'

'I could do with some pleasure,' she said.

I heard a rustle of clothing, then she knelt on the bed. She was wearing a white bra, white panties and stockings.

She leant down and kissed Tony. 'Get her to do me,' she said.

'Mmm... sounds like fun,' he chuckled.

He pulled me up off his cock and I found myself staring into the face of Jennifer Fisher. There was a time when I'd have called her my best friend. We'd been to school together. We'd shared boyfriends. Now she was obviously intent on sharing my husband too. Now I knew who the blue teddy belonged to. I tried hard not to show the slightest sign that I recognised her.

'She's got no idea, has she?' Jenny said. 'I told you Melanie's incredible. That's why I suggested you use her.'

When I heard that I almost forgot my new role. It had been her idea to have me taken to Melanie Masters. Once again I was struggling not to reveal myself and tell Jenny exactly what I thought of her. I wondered how long she'd had designs on my husband.

'I wouldn't have believed it,' Tony said. 'She's incredibly submissive. I guess that's why she got involved with that other guy. He gave her what she wanted.'

'Those nipple rings set her tits off perfectly,' Jenny cooed. 'Do you want me to have mine done?'

'Perhaps.'

'Take my knickers off, Nat.'

Eager to make sure they thought I was still completely compliant I hurried to obey. It was difficult to do such a simple thing with my hands bound behind my back, but with a lot of tugging and pulling I managed to get them down and off.

'I'm going to enjoy this,' Jenny said. 'I've always wondered what it would be like to...'

'Be careful,' Tony said. 'Her training wasn't quite finished. Her name is Nat now.'

'Don't be silly. If she had any idea she'd have realised by now, in this room. Come on, Nat, let's see what you can do.'

Jenny spread her legs apart. I had no choice but to play along. I leant forward and touched my lips against her sex, searching with my tongue. I found her clit and manipulated it, making her moan.

From lowered eyelids I saw Tony massaging her breasts. He pinched her nipples and I felt her sex contract.

'Let's make her watch us fucking. You remember all the times we had to do it in hotels?'

I almost choked. It appeared Jenny hadn't just taken advantage of my disappearance. I knew now why Tony was so disinterested in having sex with me. She'd been shagging him long before I'd started my affair.

'That's enough for the moment,' Tony said, pulling me up. 'You're to kneel on the floor and watch.'

I remembered how I'd knelt by the bed and watched him being sucked and fucked by Angela. 'Yes, master,' I said flatly. I was working out my revenge on my so-called friend. I was going to make her pay big time.

Tony lay between Jenny's legs and I watched as his cock sank into her vagina. She raised her knees, lifting her arse off the bed and allowing him to penetrate to the maximum. He began pumping into her and she grunted encouragement.

I was seething inside. It was a lot worse than I'd imagined. Tony had taken his revenge on me for having an affair whilst having one himself, and with someone I thought was a friend. In some ways it was a good job my arms were bound because the urge to hit her could so easily have overpowered me. I tried to control myself. If my plan was to succeed they had to believe I was still the submissive slave ready to do their bidding.

She was coming. She was screaming every time he pushed forward. Her fingers dug into his back, and despite my anger at what my friend had done, the sight of her being fucked so forcefully stirred my sexual appetite once again. I squeezed my thighs together and felt my clitoris respond with a sharp pulse of yearning. Despite everything I had an overwhelming desire to be fucked.

Once Jenny had come Tony rolled off her. I was glad to see his cock was still rock hard.

'You've never seen me fuck her, have you?' he said.

'No, I'd like to see that,' Jenny said dreamily, savouring the climb down from her orgasm. She reached over to the bedside cabinet, my bedside cabinet, and opened the bottom drawer where I kept my sex toys. She took out my largest dildo. Apparently my husband wasn't the only thing of mine she'd been using to fuck herself.

Tony knelt behind me and tipped me forward until my forehead was resting on the bed. He fed his cock into me, while I watched Jenny slide the dildo into her wet sex. We both moaned loudly.

The feeling of Tony's cock inside me was lovely and for a moment I could think about nothing else. But then I felt my head being pulled up by my hair. Jenny was wriggling forward with her legs on either side of my torso so her pussy was in front of my face, the base of the dildo projecting from it.

'Lick me,' she said.

I extended my tongue and found her clit. At the same time I felt his hand slide under my body and find mine. Each time he pushed forward his groin rubbed the welts he had left on my buttocks to create the delicious pain I had become so accustomed to. My anger at how the woman had betrayed me was forgotten, at least for the moment, washed away by a sea of passion.

'Don't you dare spunk in her,' Jenny said. 'Your spunk's reserved for me now.'

Tony pulled out of me.

'Now let me see you whip her,' Jenny enthused. I heard the sadistic glee in her voice.

Tony got to his feet and picked up the belt. My buttocks tingled in anticipation, and even before the belt fell my excitement mounted again.

He gave me six hard strokes across my buttocks. Each time I could not avoid a gasp of shock, gagged on Jenny's soft sex. Each time Jenny's reaction was a similar gasp, her head raised so she could see Tony's arm as it rose and fell with the belt.

'Oh yes, that's so sexy,' she encouraged.

The last stroke, my last gasp exploding against her open sex, made her come. Her body went rigid, her thighs closed around my head and her gasps became one long mewl of delight. And it made me come too. My clit, tightly cocooned between my thighs, responded to the beating with its usual enthusiasm and I orgasmed.

I wasn't sure whether Jenny pushed me away or I just fell on my side, but when I opened my eyes Tony was standing by the bed and she was sitting on the edge of it in front of him. She had moulded her breasts around his cock and was using them to masturbate him.

'Come on, give me all that lovely spunk,' she drooled.

His face creased into a rictus of bliss and spunk jetted over the tops of her breasts and her chin. She dropped her head and with her mouth drained him of every last drop.

Chapter Thirteen

I woke as the light crept around the curtains. I'd got used to sleeping in bondage and I felt refreshed and alive; it made me feel relaxed and at ease. There could be no doubt that I had a penchant for submission and all that went with it. If I had not I don't think I would have been able to keep up the pretence with Tony and Jennifer. Fortunately my peculiar sexuality had overwritten my impulse to reveal the truth.

But that did not lessen my anger with Jennifer. My so-called friend had not only seduced my husband but contrived with him to steal my inheritance, but I would get my revenge when I revealed that thanks to Jack their scheming had been foiled. I'd already selected a new managing director for my company and my husband and his mistress would be out on their ear.

But I had to be patient. If I gave them even the slightest sign that I was not totally subservient they would not take me to the meeting.

She came to get me about an hour after I'd woken up. She released me from the bed then took me into one of the guest bathrooms and locked me inside with instructions to shower and dress.

When I'd finished my ablutions she was waiting in the bedroom. She ordered me to dress. They'd laid out a plain dress, a pair of tights, knickers and a bra. The underwear was mine but not the dress. Jennifer must have bought that specially to make me look demure.

'We're going on a little trip,' she said.

'Yes, mistress,' I replied.

'Then we'll come back and see exactly what you can do.'

'I'm at your service, mistress,' I said.

'Of course you are. You have no idea, do you? I almost feel sorry for you. Almost. Now, follow me.'

The limousine was waiting outside. I recognised the driver, who said good morning to me politely, though I could see he looked surprised to see me again. I wondered how they had explained my absence.

The shareholders' meeting was being held in the conference hall across the street from the main office building. It was just about to start when Jennifer and I entered. Tony was sitting on a raised dais with the rest of the board. Fortunately for our plans Jack was a small shareholder in my company and sat with the rest of the shareholders in the room. I spotted him and Sandra sitting together towards the back.

I was taken to a chair on the dais and sat quietly while the minutes of the last meeting were read. Jenny took her seat among the shareholders. Then after two or three other items Tony announced that I had decided to agree a management buy-out in order to increase the overall profits. He was sure everyone would agree this was the best option for the future. I nodded as he spoke to give him the idea that I was agreeing. Then he produced a document for me to sign and gave me a pen.

To his astonishment I then got to my feet.

'Ladies and gentleman,' I said clearly and firmly. 'I'm afraid I'm going to have to ask your indulgence. I need to speak with Giles Foster privately for a moment.' Giles Foster was the director of finance and the man I'd selected to take over from Tony.

Giles Foster, my husband and Jenny looked astonished.

'I really don't think that's necessary,' Tony babbled. He stood in front of my chair blocking me from the view of the audience. 'You are to stop this immediately, Nat,' he hissed. 'Immediately.'

'My name is Barbara,' I said calmly. 'Now if you'll excuse me.'

I pushed him aside and indicated to Giles that he should follow me. There was absolutely nothing my husband or Jenny could do. They just had to sit there and wait.

I directed Giles into the nearest office and closed the door.

'Mr Foster, as you know I am the majority shareholder in this company. A rather awkward situation has arisen between myself and my husband and we will be getting a divorce. In order for the company to remain stable and solvent I want you to take over as managing director. Are you agreeable?'

'But this is so sudden.'

'Not really. Are you agreeable?'

'Of course. I'd be delighted. As a matter of fact I've had several problems with your husband's management style.'

'Good, let's return and tell the board the good news.'

He followed me back into the hall and up onto the dais. I saw Tony and Jenny huddled together in a corner and she was on her mobile phone. I guessed she was talking to Melanie. They wheeled around when I came back and Tony immediately stormed over.

'What are you doing? I think you need to lie down. You've not been feeling well...'

'Sit down, Tony,' I snapped, then sat in the seat he had occupied. The room went silent.

'Sorry for the delay. In fact my husband is tendering his resignation as managing director, effective immediately, and I would like the board to approve the appointment of Giles Foster as acting managing director.'

'I am doing no such thing!' Tony stormed.

'In which case I move a motion to have you dismissed, and as I am the majority shareholder your dismissal is a foregone conclusion. As you can understand from what he has just said, my husband has completely misunderstood my wishes in relation to the future of this company.'

'You just need to rest,' Tony said patronisingly. 'Now come with me.' He got up and took my arm, trying to pull me to my feet.

'This is not Melanie's house,' I said pointedly.

Giles Foster got to his feet. 'I think you should leave her alone,' he said. 'And I think you should leave the meeting right now.'

General uproar ensued. Giles called the meeting to order and suggested that the board gather to consider the developments and report back to the shareholders. As the majority shareholder I supported his proposal, and the rest made the decision unanimous.

As the meeting broke up Jack came over to my side.

'You did it,' he whispered.

'Yes I did. But there's a few other things that have got to be taken care of next, with your help, naturally.'

Chapter Fourteen

I took my champagne and walked through into the utility room where Jennifer was doing the ironing. I must say it wasn't easy for her. The leather cuffs around her wrists had been chained to a leather collar around her neck with about six inches of play between the two. This meant that to iron anything she had to lean right forward.

I preferred this position. As she was wearing a maid's uniform, in black satin with a very short skirt and petticoats bending forward revealed most of her buttocks, the tiny white triangle of her panties hardly covering anything. I preferred this because it meant I could give her encouragement with my cane without any warning.

I hit her with it then, and she shrieked.

'You've not done that very well,' I said. 'Do it again.'

'Yes Mistress Barbara,' she said quickly.

'If you don't get all the creases out you won't get any dinner,' I threatened.

I had given her a list of duties about the house; washing, cleaning, preparing meals and a timetable for their completion, even though she would often be hampered by some form of bondage. Any delays resulted in punishment by the whip.

She had no choice but to comply. Unfortunately for her, it was not only my husband she had been taking advantage of during my absence. She had been using my credit cards and bank account to buy herself a new wardrobe. We had explained to her that this was illegal and that if she didn't want to spend time in prison she would have to cooperate with our wishes.

Tony, in the meantime, suffered a similar fate. We explained to him that if we were not to report his actions to the police he should return all his share options and entitlements and leave the house with only his clothes. Which is exactly what he did.

Our revenge on Jennifer and Tony was, however, only part of our plan. After what Melanie Masters had put me through I was determined she was not going to get away with it either. Nor those who worked for her. I intended to pay them back for every stroke of the whip they had planted on my body.

Jack enlisted Tom and Sandra as we definitely needed helpers for the plan we had evolved. Judy had phoned, as she'd promised, to say she was all right and she was working things out with her husband, but I tried to ring her several times since then and never managed to get through. In fact I was very worried about her. She'd seemed so positive that she knew what she was going to do, and I just hoped nothing had gone wrong.

As Jack had found, the security at the house where Melanie operated was designed to keep the 'guests' in rather than to keep others out. So it would be relatively easy to gain admittance again. It was difficult to tell how the men and women who were being trained would react to their sudden freedom, but we sought advice from a psychologist who told us they would probably snap out of it if provided with evidence of their former lives.

We decided on a Wednesday night, or rather three o'clock in the morning on Thursday. Jack drove while Sandra, Tom and I sat expectantly. We were all dressed in black, Sandra and I in lycra catsuits and the two men in slacks and shirts. We scaled the wall with a ladder and found our way into the house easily enough. The difficult part would be finding Melanie's office. It was no good just freeing the slaves. We had to know their names and addresses and anything else about their former lives that could be used to jolt them back to reality.

In fact it wasn't as hard as we thought. Melanie's office was unlocked and her filing system was impeccable. Each slave had a file with photographs, personal details, who had brought them to Melanie and why, as well as exactly what they wanted done to them. Some had requested they be put on diets while others had wanted their prospective slaves to bulk up. Others had requested tattoos or piercings and the wives of two of the men had asked for their foreskins to be ringed so they could be chained up by them. There were daily reports on their training programmes. There were even measurements from the machines we had been made to operate so Melanie could monitor progress. Each file was also marked with the cell number of the occupant.

But as I went through the files I got a big surprise. The fifth file I opened had a photograph of Judy. For a moment I assumed it was an old file, but then I saw the date of the progress report was the day before. Clearly Judy's husband had had her returned to the house for a second attempt.

'Look, it's Judy,' I told Jack, showing him the photograph. 'She's in ten.'

'What happened?' he asked.

'I don't know but we've got to get her first.'

We took the files and made our way downstairs as quietly as we could. I felt a shudder as I walked along the corridor I had walked so many times in bondage. It wasn't entirely a shudder of fear; there was an element of excitement too.

I opened the door to ten, while Tom and Sandra stayed at the foot of the stairs in case they should hear anything.

'Judy?'

She was tied to the bed, naked. She was wearing the metal chastity belt and her hands had been strapped into leather mittens, no doubt to stop her picking the locks.

'Barbara, thank goodness. And Jack.'

'You're gorgeous,' he said, his eyes roving her naked body.

'Get me out of this,' Judy said.

'What happened?'

'I went home. I thought my husband was really contrite. He swore he'd never do anything like it again. He opened a bottle of champagne and told me he'd been a fool and begged me to forgive him. We made a toast to the future. Next thing I remember I woke up back here, tied hand and foot. It's been hell. They've had me in this cell listening to that strange sound 24/7. I've been going nuts.'

They untied her and she stretched her limbs in relief.

'We've come to get Madam M,' I said. .

'Get her?'

'She can't be allowed to get away with what she's done.'

'What, the police you mean?' Judy asked.

'We had something a little more imaginative in mind,' Jack said. 'How many others are there? Barbara thought there were four.'

'There are, but only Celine and Angel live in.'

'Good, we should be able to take care of them without any trouble as there's five of us.'

'I need to find some clothes,' Judy said.

We went out into the corridor. There were the cupboards full of rubber clothing but Judy said she'd prefer to wait until she found something a little less uncomfortable. But we helped ourselves to cuffs and bondage gear of all sorts; ropes, gags and blindfolds, which would be useful later on.

Stealthily we climbed the stairs and investigated the corridors on the first floor. It seemed clear that Melanie's bedroom was on this floor so we decided to go to the second floor first to neutralise any threat from the two associates. The rooms on the second floor were clearly smaller. We went along a narrow corridor opening doors quietly one by one. It wasn't until we got to the fourth that we found a bedroom that was occupied. It was Angel's bedroom. She was sleeping, lying under a single sheet.

We crept inside without disturbing her, and took up position around the bed. At my signal we pounced on her, each grabbing a limb while Jack clamped a hand over her mouth. It was essential we didn't let her scream.

She started awake and struggled but was no match for the five of us. Hurriedly we jammed a gag into her mouth, then twisted her over onto her back and secured her arms and legs with rope. As an extra security measure we used more rope to tie her to the bed, then slipped a blindfold over her eyes. One down and two to go.

Judy helped herself to something from Angel's wardrobe. She dressed in a leather V-neck top and a short leather skirt. Even Angel's calf-length boots fitted her. I saw Jack watching as she pulled the clothes on and I found myself staring too, remembering the long nights I'd spent playing with that lush, pliable body.

We left Angel and proceeded along the corridor to the next door. There were two more empty rooms before we found Celine. We practised the same procedure, surrounding the bed before seizing her and stuffing a gag in her mouth. She was then as securely tied as Angel had been.

Now came Madam M. We crept downstairs and along the first floor corridor to double doors that obviously led to the master bedroom. But it appeared it was not going to be as easy to surprise Melanie as the others. Coming from behind the double doors were the unmistakable sounds of loud lovemaking.

'She's not alone,' I whispered.

'We haven't any choice,' Jack said. I opened the door as quietly as I could. I had been wrong. Melanie was alone and was going to be very surprised.

What we saw astonished us all. The bedroom was elaborately decorated with a large bed. There was a sofa and a table and chairs, but what drew all our eyes was the contraption to one side. It was like a narrow vaulting horse padded in black leather with four splayed legs, and she was lying prone and naked on it with her ankles strapped into cuffs attached to the bottom of the legs. On the other two legs, at the same level, were two handles which she was gripping fiercely. Her hair, always pinned severely to her head, was loose and almost swept the carpet.

But that was not the most unusual bit. Behind the frame was a substantial metal box with electric wires leading into it. Extending from the box was a metal rod, on the end of which was a silicon phallus in a natural skin colour. I could not tell how long it was exactly because it was being driven in and out of Melanie's cunt, by whatever mechanism the box contained. It and her pussy lips were glistening with her juices, and she was so absorbed in her activities she didn't hear us come in. I judged she was near to her orgasm, and as she had denied me mine so many times I thought it only fair to do the same to her. I pulled the plug of the machine out of the socket. Silence descended. Melanie raised her head.

'What the fuck are you doing?'

She tried to get up but Jack grabbed her hands and pulled them back to the handles, quickly tying them in place with rope.

'We've come to spend a little quality time with you,' I said. I stroked her tanned buttocks, the muscles taut and well exercised. Her sex was completely shaved, her labia glistening with juices.

'I'm sure you'll enjoy it,' Judy added.

'I certainly will,' Jack said. The sight of Melanie in such a vulnerable position clearly excited him and I saw a bulge in his trousers.

'Be my guest,' I said. I went over to the machine and pulled it away from her, the phallus popping out of her vagina with an audible sucking sound.

'I'll get you for this,' she swore.

'Oh that's much too loud,' Jack said. He took one of the inflatable gags we'd brought up from the cellar and was about to push it into her mouth when Tom intervened. 'I've got something that will be just as effective,' he said. He unzipped his trousers. It wasn't only Jack affected by Melanie's prone body. Tom's cock was semi-erect.

We all grinned. There was a time when this sort of spectacle would have shocked me. But now, after what Melanie had put me through, I was delighted to see her getting the sort of treatment she had meted out to us. Tom positioned himself in front of her and pulled her face up by the hair. She made no attempt to turn away as he forced his cock between her lips.

Judy had a whip in her hand, taken from a selection she'd found. Melanie tried to protest but the words were muffled on Tom's erection. Judy raised her arm and the first stroke thwacked down on the white flesh of Melanie's buttocks, making it quiver and raising an immediate line of red.

'How does it feel?' Judy asked as she whipped her again, though she knew she wouldn't get a reply.

I went over to Jack and unzipped his slacks, easing his erection out of his pants. I wanked him and felt a sharp pulse of desire.

'Leave some for me,' I said, caressing the helmet of his glans with my fingers, rubbing the tear of liquid that had formed there into his shiny globe.

He grasped Melanie by the hips and pushed his cock towards her sex. It was obvious the whipping had excited her, and as Jack began to pound into her, the position she offered perfect for the maximum penetration, Tom moved away to lie on the bed with Sandra on one side and Judy on the other. Judy was immediately busy sucking his cock while Sandra was kissing his balls. He had his left hand under Judy's skirt and his right between Sandra's legs, the zip of the catsuit open. While I watched he pulled himself up and rolled Judy onto her back, pushing her skirt up and exposing her shaven slit. As his cock disappeared into her Sandra squirmed round and began kissing her.

I turned back to Melanie. Again she was on the brink of an orgasm. Sweat was coating her naked body and she was moaning and gasping in time with Jack's powerful thrusts. One or two more strokes from him would have finished her off but I was determined she would suffer as I had done.

I grabbed his waist and pulled him back. She gasped as his cock slid out of her.

'Please, please... don't stop...' she gasped.

'My turn,' I said. I positioned him right in front of her eyes, then slid to my knees and sucked his cock into my mouth. I sucked him and played with his cock with my tongue, licking Melanie's juices off. He had already been on the brink as he'd fucked Melanie and now, with my hand playing with his balls, I felt his cock jerk violently. I wanted to make it as bad for her as I could so when I heard his moans of pleasure reaching a crescendo I pulled him out of my mouth and used my nimble fingers to direct his jets of spunk onto Melanie's face. She gasped as the pearly liquid hit her cheek and began to slide down towards her hair.

I told Jack to unzip my catsuit, and quickly peeled it off. I knew what I wanted. I wanted to try the machine Melanie had been using. I'd never seen anything like it before. Jack and I examined it together. It was completely adjustable and could be regulated by a remote control to go slower or faster as desired.

Jack suggested I knelt on all fours on the floor, while he lowered the equipment until the plastic phallus was at the right height. Then pulling my panties aside, I gingerly backed onto it. My wet sex opened willingly. Slowly I moved back further. When the flared base was pressing against my labia Jack handed me the remote control. It had a dial numbered from one to ten. I turned it to five. Jack knelt beside my head and began playing with my breasts, massaging them and pinching my nipples. I was so turned on I barely registered that the others had stopped their games and were crowding around me on the floor, keen to watch as the relentless machine brought me to a shattering orgasm. My juices were making a squelching sound every time the phallus drove into me, and that fuelled my excitement. The remote dropped from my hand but Jack picked it up, and as he turned the machine up to full power I orgasmed almost immediately, screaming out my pleasure as the others watched.

He stopped the machine and I pulled myself off it, exhausted and entirely satisfied. But I wasn't finished with Melanie. I wanted her to experience more of what she'd put us through.

'Let's use it on her,' I said.

The others agreed. The machine was readjusted so the tip of the phallus, still glistening from my juices, was butting into Melanie's perfectly positioned sex. The marks the whip left on her buttocks had darkened and was almost purple. I couldn't resist caressing them and she gasped.

Jack started the machine. She gasped again and shook her head, lifting it to beg us to stop. But she couldn't hold her head there for long and dropped it down, as the phallus pumped into her at half speed. Jack turned the control up to maximum and Melanie's body reacted by arching off the bench. As she settled back she began to fuck the machine just as much as it was fucking her, riding the cock back and forth, though her movement was limited by her bondage.

As her excitement increased I nodded to Jack, who knew exactly what I intended. He immediately cut the power of the machine.

'No...!' Melanie screamed.

She tried to push herself back onto the phallus more forcibly but could do little more than wriggle her hips. I knelt beside her head and pulled it up so she was looking straight into my eyes. Her face was full of frustration, just as mine had been.

'You don't get off that easily.'

I pushed the machine away and caressed her buttocks, concentrating on the welts Judy's whipping had left. Melanie shuddered under my touch. Slowly, gently I smooth my fingers down until they were touching her wet pussy lips.

Judy picked up one of the gags we'd brought from the cellar and stuffed it unceremoniously into Melanie's mouth, strapping it tightly in place. I slipped my fingers into her vagina and found her clit. Delicately, careful not to push her over the boundary into an orgasm, I teased it with the ball of my thumb.

We were doing to her what she had frequently done to us. We kept her on the brink of orgasm but never let her over it. In front of her she could not help but watch Jack, who had taken over from Tom and was fucking Sandra on the bed, giving her a string of orgasms, each one louder and more shattering than the last, until he lost control and sprayed his spunk over her buttocks.

Carefully I stroked Melanie's clit while Judy tormented her nipples and breasts, pinching them, pulling them, kneading them.

'Beg me,' I whispered in her ear.

'Ah...' she managed to say through the gag. It did sound a little like please.

'Can't hear you,' I taunted.

'Ah...' she mumbled again.

'No sorry, I'm not in the mood.' I pulled my fingers away.

'No...' Melanie screamed into the gag.

'Oh yes,' I said. 'We're in control of everything you do now.'

Judy wrapped her arms around my waist. She cupped my naked breasts in her hands. We rolled together onto the bed and my mouth pressed to her sex while hers was doing the same to mine.

As I orgasmed under her tongue I looked to the side to see the desperate frustration in Melanie's eyes; the same frustration she had so often made me feel. That revenge was sweet.

They pulled Melanie down the stairs and into the cell Barbara had occupied. She seemed docile enough, accepting the fact that there was nothing she could do to stop them attaching the metal chastity belt around her waist and between her legs, before tying her hand and foot to the bed.

In the morning, after they'd found accommodation in the house, with Judy, Barbara and Jack sharing Melanie's bedroom, while Tom went off with Sandra, they went down into the cellar to release the unwitting 'guests'.

While they wandered about looking bemused, Jack found the equipment used to play the strange sounds in the middle of the night, and destroyed it.

By the second day all those who had been held captive began to regain at least a sketchy outline of what had happened to them and why, though for some it took longer than others.

One of the first female slaves to recover her memory had the brilliant idea of forcing Melanie to get her husband to come to the house on some pretext or other. When he arrived he was locked into one of the cells to experience what she had gone through. Judy and Barbara were keen to take part and even dressed in Celine and Angel's bizarre rubber costumes, while the poor man was given hell by them and his wife.

Others heard of this idea and demanded the same treatment for the partners who'd had them imprisoned, so by the end of the week, when everyone had recovered their faculties, the cells were full with the would-be masters and the two would-be mistresses who'd paid Melanie to train their spouses. The revenge was perfect. The only difference from the previous regime's treatment was these inmates knew what they had done and why they were there.

Slowly Melanie's house of punishment was rundown. Her office had revealed more secrets; the names and addresses of all her previous 'patients', the women and men who were presumably now living as slaves, kowtowing to their master's or mistresses' every whim. It was going to be difficult but Barbara knew looking up these households was going to be the next thing on her agenda. She had a feeling there were going to be some very interesting encounters, and of course, she would be happy to offer her special expertise in ensuring that the revenge the slaves dished out when they discovered the truth was just as excruciating as their experiences at the hands of Melanie Masters.

Becky Bell's THE DOMINATRIX is also available as a paperback on AMAZON.

A man stood on tiptoe in the middle of the room, his arms stretched up above his head. His wrists had been strapped into a pair of padded leather cuffs which were tied to a white nylon rope, threaded through a pulley above his head and tied off on a cleat on the nearest wall. His entire body was encased in tight black rubber, including his head, which had been crammed into a rubber helmet. The helmet had only one tiny hole presently open, at the base of his nostrils. His legs were bound together by thick rubber straps at his ankles and above his knees. A large erection pushed out against the rubber that covered his belly...

Paula Divine is a woman who takes her pleasures very seriously. As a top dominatrix, she spends her days and nights in a uniform of cruel high heels and jet-black basque, teasing and chastising a procession of hapless men who are more than happy to pay for the privilege of being her slave.

And unlike most women in her line of work, Paula enjoys inflicting pain and humiliation just as much as her clients enjoy receiving it. For her, nothing is quite so arousing as the sight of a naked man, bound and helpless, pleading for mercy.

But Paula has just discovered something to add zest to even her feverish sex life. A young, innocent estate agent called Angela, who finds the business of domination almost as exciting as the prospect of sex with another, older and far more experienced woman.

www.ingramcontent.com/pod-product-compliance
Lightning Source LLC
Chambersburg PA
CBHW070805120626
46557CB00002B/719